DEAD DOG BEACH

by

P J Murdoch

Published by Neetah Books

First printing: June 2025

A CIP catalogue for this title is available from the British Library.

ISBN: 978-1-908898-63-0

ACKNOWLEDGEMENTS

A massive shout out to Mary Irvine, for taking the time to keep me right. To John O'Hare, for his advice, life-long friendship and continued support as my roadie. To Graham Morgan MBE for being my first Guinea pig reader. To Gordon Wallace for always believing in this story. To all my old bandmates – honest, none of these characters are you! And to my family – I love you all so much. I hope you'll keep on rockin' long after I'm gone.

CHAPTER ONE

Maria was very hard to please. Whether it was an anniversary, a birthday, or even Christmas Day, you had to have a few options up your sleeve just in case the first offering wasn't quite up to scratch. She was from fiery, Italian stock, and she knew what she wanted. She knew what I wanted too. Or at least she thought she did...

"I know what you want," she said. "You want a 'yes-lady', someone who will glow when you succeed." She smiled to herself without taking her eyes off the starched tablecloth. "They'll trot along to every one of your little gigs and clap harder than anyone else."

"I've not played a gig in years, Maria," I mumbled.

Maria trailed the heavy silver fork across the pressed linen and then watched the four parallel lines fade back into the cloth. She sighed, lifted her head as if it were made out of solid lead and said, "It's time to do what we said we always would."

I glanced across at the other tables, all smiles and giggles, oblivious to my growing anxiety.

I could feel my face getting hotter, erupting pore by pore into what I'm sure would be a very noticeable 'beamer'.

Maria was going to drop a bomb, and there was bound to be collateral damage. I looked again to see if anyone was listening. "What exactly did we say we would always do?"

"You know, fine well," she snapped.

I whispered the next few words, sharp and straight, as if I had two seconds before a firing squad let rip, "Maria, this meal is costing us a fortune."

Maria lifted her fork until it was level with my nose. She held it like a matador. "We were right when we said that we should go our separate ways after ten years."

My head began replaying a drunken scene from a beach in Sardinia. "I presumed that was just... "

"Just what, Ian?" she interrupted.

"—a load of crap spouted out by a couple of young kids on a stupid beach," I parried. I was under attack. One of those unprovoked attacks that you couldn't prepare for. I began looking around the restaurant in desperation, wishing we'd never come.

"What's wrong, Ian? Are you frightened your fans will get to see you with your guard down?"

"Don't be silly," I protested. But she was right. I hated public barneys. My misery was nobody's business but mine. I'd walked out of better places than this, rather than get a barrage of abuse in front of a crowd of people I didn't even know.

"What about sticking to the plan?" she pressed, in the kind of raised tone that meant business.

Several heads turned towards our table.

"It wasn't a bloody plan," I hissed as quietly as I could. "It was a drunken, immature promise that we never had any intention of keeping."

"Not for me it wasn't. And…" She noticed the waiter moving towards the table, "now it makes perfect sense."

I felt like I'd just been sentenced to a particularly nasty form of crucifixion. "What the hell are you doing? We're having our anniversary dinner."

"Pre-anniversary dinner," Maria corrected.

In a last-ditch attempt, I adopted a pleading tone, "This is the best restaurant in town. You said…"

"Never mind what I said," interrupted Maria, "we both know that you'd be much happier with a young Asian wife. Don't you remember?"

I struggled to remember anything. "What are you on about now?"

"Your pal Googled one. What's his name? The manager of the Ox and Bow."

"What's Harry-bloody-Finch got to do with anything?" I hissed. "The man's a complete twat!"

"And now he's got himself a perfect little twat, according to his ex-wife, Doreen."

"Doreen?" I was beginning to boil. Now it was me. I had to stay calm but was no logic here, nothing to hold on to.

Maria rummaged in her brown, chequered handbag for a second before producing a very tattered-looking piece of card.

She read from it: "No relationship should last more than 10 years. Quote: 'Every marriage certificate should have an expiry date." Maria crumpled the message into a small ball and then threw it straight at my face.

I winced as it pinged off my forehead.

"Your own words," she reminded.

"Written on the back of a beer mat…" I hissed, retrieving the crumpled beer mat from the carpet. "… ten years ago. We were rat-arsed."

A waiter hovered, nervously, about five feet from our table, his tray brimming with a sumptuous array of seafood and samphire.

Without even looking, Maria fluttered her fingers at him in a 'just wait there' kind of way.

This was no joke. She was actually going to ruin the meal–our anniversary–and the rest of my life. "What do you want me to say, Maria?" I pleaded.

Maria closed her eyes. "We agreed."

"No we didn't."

"Yes we did," she persisted.

"Excuse me, Madame," squeaked the waiter.

"What?" snapped Maria.

"Your starter?" He strained under the weight of the heavy silver tray which he held at a dangerously awkward, angle.

Again, without even looking at him, Maria waved a finger of warning. "Admit it, Ian! You don't want to be with me any more either, do you?"

I glanced up at the waiter and noticed a large bead of sweat splash onto our seafood.

"No... I mean, yes." I was trying to piece something together. A line of genius that would get us back on track.

The waiter tried to move in again, but Maria stopped him in his tracks with a piercing stare.

Breathing heavily, he edged back a few inches. A vein on his left temple pulsed rhythmically.

"Why won't you admit it?"

"Please?" I whispered. "Not here?"

"Admit you want out too," she pressed, loudly.

I was floundering badly. "Can't we just have dinner, and then I'll admit anything you want?"

The waiter nodded his agreement.

"Don't you dare," hissed Maria.

I glanced up at the waiter unsure if she was chastising him or me.

She took a deep breath and then waved the waiter forward.

The waiter issued a small squeak of relief and dashed for the table.

Maria picked at the samphire before letting her fork drop with a loud clank onto the plate. "I want someone who actually wants to be with me, who doesn't disappear downstairs at 6am, like some creeping Jesus. I hate waking up alone. I'm more alone when you're home than when you're away! Here." Maria could have taken off her rings or slipped me a lawyer's letter, but she did something far worse; she unclipped her gold necklace and let an ornate, brass key slip free of the chain. This wasn't any old key; it was *our* key. It sparkled on the bleached linen as the wine waiter came into view. We'd chosen the tasting menu, so there was a different glass with every course.

"The Champagne to start, sir?" The sommelier caressed the elegant bottle as if it were his lover. He leaned into the table and raised his eyebrows expectantly.

Again, Maria pushed the bottle away without even a glance and looked me straight in the eye. "You were right," she said, sliding the key towards me, "all those years ago, you knew how it was going to be. I kept the key so I wouldn't forget ... so you wouldn't forget our pact."

"It was really your idea... the pact. The whole ten years' thing; not mine," I explained.

"Don't start re-writing history, Ian."

I looked down at the table. "I said it was the key to your heart."

Just for a moment, Maria softened. "You did." She bit down, ever so softly, on her bottom lip. "You were romantic back then."

"I still am," I reasoned. "Look around you. We are about to eat the best food money can buy."

"You can't buy romance, Ian. Do you remember where that beach was? Where I got the key?"

"Sardinia," I muttered.

She nodded. "Dead Dog Beach."

The sommelier raised his eyebrows and glanced down at his bottle.

Maria took a deep exasperated breath and said, "I feel empty inside, Ian."

I wanted to say something but I couldn't think what.

"You need someone to look after you in your old age," she assured me. Then, with a derisory little shake of her head, she said, "That person isn't me."

"Old age?" I spluttered. "I'm only thirty-two." This time I halted the sommelier before he attempted another sortie, anger drifting over me like a warm tropical mist. "Just tell me what you want me to do, Maria."

"I shouldn't have to tell you. You should know." Maria clenched her fists and said, in a voice far too loud for such a small, intimate venue, "I want out!"

I thought she was going to begin shouting, I mean, really belting it out, but it was worse than that, she began sobbing. Big tears were rolling down her face, dripping onto her crumpled napkin.

Three couples began shifting food around the plates, pretending not to watch. At another table, a group of young girls, out on some celebration by the look of the cards and presents, stopped laughing.

"Maria," I begged, "it's our anniversary."

"It's all wrong!" she shouted.

"But–"

"No."

"I could–"

"No!"

"Just let me–"

"I said no!" she snapped. Her tears vanished as she dug her nails into the rosemary and sea salt bread roll.

It was at this point that I decided it was time to switch from being pleading and placatory to being full-on manly and assertive. There was no way back now anyway, so with a tight jaw I spoke slowly, quietly and precisely, "You know something, Maria, this is nothing to do with any stupid pact. I let you into my life at a time–"

"Fuck off, Ian!" she spat. "How many times have I heard this?

How many times has anyone who will listen to you heard about you and your big hit single? And how you just needed a bit more time to write one more ... to write another fuckin' classic in an attic. I supported you!"

This was way below the belt. A dagger in the heart. "We go on holiday every year on the royalties!"

"A shit holiday!" The delicate bread roll disintegrated between her fingers.

I drew back and waited.

"The wine, sir?" pressed the sommelier, in a high, expectant voice.

I glanced first at the panic-stricken sommelier and then at Maria. "Now, Maria, stay calm. There are people trying to have a nice meal."

"Fuck them!" she blasted.

I suddenly remembered that telling Maria to stay calm was about as wise as kicking Attila the Hun in the nuts.

"You selfish arse!" she yelled.

The restaurant rang with the clinking of cutlery.

Maria narrowed her eyes and stood up. I watched the sommelier stagger back several feet.

He bumped back against an empty table yet shielded his wine as if it were a new-born.

"You..." She pointed straight at me, "you are so far up your own arse that you will never see the light!"

The sommelier swivelled round on his heels and retreated, while the rest of the diners just stared, open-mouthed.

She began to walk away.

"Wait a minute!" I whispered, as loudly as I could.

Maria came to a halt before she reached the door.

She turned back to face me, wiggling her forefinger like a magic wand, her mouth open, poised, ready to unleash one final tirade.

I felt sick.

To my utter relief she faked a smile and then gave me one of her best 'you're not worth it' looks.

Like Wimbledon, I noticed heads turning from one to the other. Everyone was waiting to see what kind of return I would make, but... there was nothing left inside me apart from a dark, empty space. I fumbled to pick the abandoned key from the tablecloth.

"Game, set and match to the lady," whispered a man with a rounded belly.

His partner elbowed him in the ribs.

Maria put on her coat and left while I, determined to shut out the whole world, placed the key in my pocket and then proceeded to toy with her discarded napkin.

The maître d' suddenly arrived with the bill on a silver platter. "Sir?"

I had lost my appetite and actually wavered on the edge of consciousness when I saw the £269.52 total. It included a 15% discretionary service charge, a £5 donation to Battersea Dog Home and a wishful little mission statement that read–'We aim to please'.

"She'll be back," whispered the maître d', with a nod and a wink.

I looked at him carefully. "Yeah, sure she will. With a spring in her step and a song in her fucking heart."

The maître d' took my credit card. "See, that's more like it. Chin up."

I had never felt like punching someone in the face so much in my whole life.

CHAPTER TWO

As soon as I reached the door of the restaurant I was overcome with a pang of remorse. At least I thought it was remorse until I replayed Maria's words in my head. She'd planned this ambush, knew how is would play out... that I'd be humiliated. A rage—an anger that I hadn't felt for years coursed through me.

I had to go after her. Give her a real piece of my mind. Why should she have the last say?

I began to run down the plush hotel stairs, past a blur of people all standing in little annoying clusters that blocked my way. I weaved through them like a rugby winger at the top of his game. Any of those happy bastards that didn't move quick enough would get a quick shove, a jab in the ribs ... Fuck them all! Fuck the whole world. I was going to reach Maria before she escaped this time, and I didn't care who I had to–

"Hey!" A woman with an American accent threw her drink up into the air as I ducked under her, but I didn't care. I could see the grand double doors that marked the front of the hotel. I pushed onwards and threw them open.

Maria was just getting into a taxi about fifty yards away. I shouted at the top of my voice – "Well, fuck off then! You can stick your marriage right up your big fat arse!" She didn't have a fat arse, but that wasn't the point.

As her taxi pulled away, a cold blast of air ruffled my hair. My eyes cleared, and there I was– standing at the top of the steps. A girl in a white dress and a young man in a kilt right beside me, their mouths open in surprise. A crowd below the steps had their cameras and phones held up like it was a rock concert. People behind the door I'd just pushed open were spilling out into the sunshine.

I turned to the bride and automatically glanced down at her arse. My final rant at Maria still fresh in my mind. "No ..." I began. "I wasn't taking about your arse ..."

The groom's eyes narrowed. I felt a hand grab my shoulder. "Are you quite finished, boy?" Again, an angry, American accent caught my attention. The man was huge and bald.

"I …" I didn't know what to say. There seemed to be a thousand people staring at me as if I was the worst kind of scum. As if I'd just eaten a live, fluffy kitten in front of a bunch of vegans and given the 'thumbs up'.

The American's fingers gripped me harder. His red, glistening head moving closer to mine.

"Ian?"

I recognised this voice.

"What are you doing here?" it continued.

"I'll tell you what he's doing here," roared the bald American. "He is trying to ruin my daughter's wedding!"

"Leave him to me. I'll get him out of your way."

It was Andy Miller. The drummer in my last band. In fact, the drummer in every band I'd ever been in other than the one that mattered.

The American pushed me away. "Well, you better, or I'll–"

"Give him a good kicking?" said Andy, in his usual cockney sing-song voice. "And who could blame you, mate? Leave this prick to me."

Andy caught me by the sleeve of my jacket and hauled me back into the hotel, through the throng of family and friends that had come to see that bride. I noticed the big American lady, the one I'd ducked under on my mad dash, staring at my ass. She gave me a lurid wink. I turned to Andy. "Did you see that?"

"That's the Mother of the Bride. Keep moving."

I felt the sleeve of my jacket rip. "Hey!"

Andy stopped.

We seemed to be out of harm's way. I examined my jacket. "This is an Armani jacket–"

"That you got for a fiver from the charity shop in Bearsden," he finished.

I hated it when Andy cut me down like that. "That's not the point."

I wondered why Andy had appeared. Emerging out of the blue like some Marvel hero, to snatch me away from certain death. But then I saw the open doors ahead and the stage at the far end of the ball room. "You're playing?"

"Yes, Ian. Some of us aren't supported by a well-off wife who …" He hesitated and stared straight into my eyes. "Who seem to have come to their senses at last."

I could feel the anger rising in my chest again. "You are such a nosey bastard, Andy."

Andy laughed. "Nosey? Over a hundred people saw her take off, and you … shouting after her like that. What a wanker."

"You don't know the full story. We had a row," I said.

Andy let me go and stood back. "I gathered." He suddenly looked down at the carpet and picked up a key.

I snatched it off him. "That's mine."

"So is this." He added, handing me a white envelope.

I took it from him. "What's this?"

"Maria gave it to me as she was making her escape. Said that she forgot to give you it."

A wave of embarrassment wafted over me. I stuffed the envelope and the key into my jacket pocket.

"Look," said Andy, "I need to play a couple of sets but I can give you a lift home after if you like?"

"No," I replied. I didn't want Andy's false pity. "I'll grab a drink at the other bar and head off later."

Andy shrugged. "Suit yourself. But I'd keep a low profile if I was you."

* * *

Two pints later I decided to wander back to the front desk and call a taxi. I'd calmed down a little but I still hadn't opened the letter Maria had given to Andy. I was distracted for a moment by the whoops and wails of the wedding party and was just about to turn the corner to reception when a familiar voice said, "Hi! It's you!"

The words tore a hole in my self-pity. I had shame, embarrassment and revenge all spinning round in my head and I really wanted to let them whir round a little longer before I had to speak to anyone.

I replied in an unsteady voice, "You're the …"

"Mother of the-Bride," she slurred.

I was trying to pinpoint her American accent.

She winked at me for the second time that day, and said, "You owe me a drink." She hiccupped and reached out for a nearby door handle to steady herself.

Alabama or Georgia I decided. She had a drawl that made me think of some glam-puss out of *Gone With the Wind*.

"I'm going home," I ventured, half-hoping she would slide down the wall and fall asleep.

"Shame, cause I like Scottish mans… men…" she giggled at her own mistake.

I nodded in a kind of 'whatever you say' kind of way.

"My husband hates you!" She narrowed her eyes and began scanning the hallway for any sign of him. "But he's a shit," she continued, 'And…" She peered about her again, "he's not here." She let out a big puff of air and then quickly covered her mouth. Her eyes widened in desperation.

The ladies' toilets were right behind me, so I guided her to the door.

The sounds of music and merriment continued to ooze down the corridor, and it occurred to me that if I could just find another woman to help this amorous American, I could sneak off into the night.

There was a sharp screech, a thump and then a sexy giggle as the Mother of the Bride literally fell into the ladies and lay flat on her face. Her black dress had wrinkled up around the top of her legs.

"Are you alright?" I whispered, trying not to look.

A pair of partially stockinged legs made sure that the door of the ladies' toilet was now impossible to close.

I should have left her there. I really should have. But, stupidly, I scrambled over her and tried my best to pull her all the way inside. This, I decided, was the lesser of two evils, as I didn't want to be caught hauling her out of the ladies, flat-out, and half-naked.

To my relief, she slid fairly effortlessly along the moist, piss-covered floor. The door swung shut behind us.

It was then that she chose to become semi-lucid. My hands still gripping hers, she smiled a drunken smile and, it must be said, somewhat surprisingly, swivelled up onto her knees with the svelteness of a ballerina.

"You better cover yourself up," I whispered. I could see, in a little mirror positioned on the inside of the door, that her backside was on full display. We were all alone in the ladies.

I pulled my hands free of her grip, raised them in surrender and backed away. "Now, look..."

She slurred 'kiss me' and started slithering towards me across the piss-covered floor like some slime-monster out of Dr Who. Shame I didn't have a T.A.R.D.I.S to duck into.

The loo door swished open behind her and a party of three giggling girls pushed their way inside. They instantly stopped laughing when they saw me. I could almost hear their minds whizzing round to the wrong conclusion.

"She felt sick," I protested.

"Never mind that, you should see the view we have from here," snapped the nearest girl. She was skinny with pointy elbows and an even sharper expression.

"Can you help?" I broached.

"Maybe he's her husband," hissed a tall blonde with a bob. She wore a low-cut, gold-lamé mini dress and sported a tattoo of a swallow on her left breast.

"No chance," said a girl with grey-feathered fascinator. It looked as though an parrot had committed hari-kari by flying straight into the side of her head.

"I'm not her husband," I explained, limply.

"He's my lover," she blasted, waving the girls away as if they were slaves.

"What?" I bleated.

The girl with the fascinator simply stepped around the bare-arsed Mother of the Bride and said, "For fuck's sake, get a room!"

As she and one of the other girls found an empty cubicle, there was a loud knock from outside in the corridor.

I waited as the blonde with the bob staggered back to the door and peered outside. "Yes?" she said, sounding like a grumpy receptionist. "You're who?" she continued.

I couldn't hear the other side of the conversation as the band was busy pounding out *Sweet Caroline*. Drunken 'whow ... oh ... ohs' echoed into the toilets like a war chant.

"Well," said the blonde with the bob, "if you are who you say you are, your wife is in here … with no knickers on," she added, unhelpfully.

"Jesus!" I wailed.

The door swung inward and the blonde with the bob stepped aside to reveal the angry, bald American. His red face had the same expression he'd sported earlier–like a bulldog chewing on a wasp.

I made out the words 'dead meat' and 'rip your head off' as I retreated. My back bumped against a hard porcelain sink.

"Go on," goaded the girl with the skinny elbows, she was peering over the top of her cubicle, "let him have it!"

"I was only trying to help," I protested.

"Haven't you done enough today, you little bastard?" he growled.

He caught my lapel with his left hand and threw a punch with his right.

My head cracked off the mirror behind me and a blinding white light swallowed me whole. Strangely, I could still hear stuff. Mainly, the American shouting at his wife, which was good as it meant he was probably finished with me.

I lay completely still and must have drifted in and out of consciousness because the next thing I remember was cold water being poured over my face.

"Wake up!"

I could only open one eye and instinctively covered my face with my forearms.

Another lash of cold water almost drowned me.

"Look at the state of you."

"Andy?" I was struggling to see out of my one good eye.

Andy Miller was holding an empty crystal vase that dripped green, fowl-smelling water. I don't know how I got there but I was sitting on a chair at the side of the stage. His drums had been dismantled and the ballroom was empty.

"You're going to have a shiner," he chuckled, pointing at my closed eye.

I tried to stand up and felt a sharp pain at the back of my head. Tentatively, I patted my hair and then looked at my hand. There were traces of dried blood.

"So, let me get this straight," continued Andy, "Maria is only gone five minutes and you try it on with the Mother of the Bride in the bogs?"

"No, I … "

"It's lucky we had a break. Some girl remembered we played in bands together. She told me you were in trouble."

"She must have a good memory."

"Anyway, I managed to get you away from the Tyson lookalike and sit you on that chair at the side of the stage, where I could keep an eye on you."

It was then that I spied the white envelope in Andy's shirt pocket. I patted my jacket pocket. "Is that my letter?"

"Oh, yes. Here."

I ripped it out of his hand. "And you've read it."

"Of course I bloody read it." he pressed. "It sounds like you're off the hook? A free man."

I glowered at him. "You'd love that, wouldn't you?"

"What? You and me playing in a band again, having a ball?" He slipped on his coat. "Nah, I'd hate it."

"I need to get back home, Andy." He always was a nosy bastard. He hated it when I got married. He hated it even more when I joined another band and had a hit record.

"I told you I could give you a lift. That's if you're not too proud to ride in a van these days," Andy added.

He was actually excited by our split. I could see it in his beady little eyes. He'd got divorced a year back and now he thought it was just going to be like old times.

"I can get a taxi," I said.

"Don't be daft," he snapped. "I've covered your arse, so you can help me lift my gear into the van."

I let out a pained sigh. Why the hell did Maria have to involve him in our fall out? Of all the people on the planet, why had she given Andy the bloody letter? I didn't even know what was in it myself yet. He seemed to read my mind as he struggled with the fire exit.

"The letter just said that you made some pact to split and that she was calling you in on it. She said it would be best if she went back to her family."

As we made our way in and out of the empty function hall, I stopped to survey the familiar scene. Streamers and poppers littered the dance floor as a few weary-looking barmen gathered up the empty glasses from the tables. The sprung, spruce floor was sticky with spilled drink and the air in the room had a sharp tang to it.

"Not the same, is it?" said Andy. He pulled a bundle of shining drum stands off the stage.

I cupped my arms until he'd finished loading me up.

"I preferred the smell of stale smoke to the ming you get these days: carbolic and disinfectant."

My head throbbed as I lowered the metal stands into the back of the van. On my way back to the stage, I picked up a clean burgundy serviette from the buffet table and filled it with a half dozen cold sausage rolls and a few chicken drumsticks.

Andy smiled and said, "Old habits die hard."

Typical Andy, always the more aggressive scavenger when it came to left-overs, he gathered up twice as much as I did in a poly bag, probably taken along for this very purpose. Then, with a wink, he retrieved two unopened bottles, from behind a curtain. "Bastards just throw it out anyway."

"Not two bottles of unopened champagne they fuckin' don't," I added.

"Whatever." He nodded at a tired-looking waiter in the corner. "Those little twats probably have a side-line selling it off. There's no way the Father of the Bride can keep an eye on every bottle."

I shook my head. "You really are a thieving bastard."

"Opportunistic."

"Thieving!" I repeated.

Outside I moaned, sliding into the passenger seat. I bit into the first of the sausage rolls. It tasted fantastic but any pleasure was soon dulled by the thought of what had happened that night. I watched Andy pop one of the bottles and take a large swig. He almost choked on the bubbles.

"You're driving," I reminded.

"When did that ever stop us?" He handed me the bottle and revved up the Ford Transit.

I saw his teeth flash in the moonlight as he bit down on an onion bhaji.

CHAPTER THREE

By the time we'd reached the house, the pain from the cut at the back of my head was beginning to ease. We'd polished off the first bottle of champers and most of the sausage rolls on the way, and Andy managed to tell me a little more about his encounter with Maria. He said she looked worried, almost scared when he'd met her. I could understand, upset or angry—even sad—but not 'scared'.

Andy let the van roll down the driveway of my semi-detached until the front bumper kissed the garage door. "You've got an empty!" he exclaimed.

"Maybe," I said, still unsure whether Maria was in the house or not.

"She's well-gone." He held up the second bottle of Taittinger and smiled. "Gone for good, I reckon."

"What a great friend you are, Andy. A helpful hand in times of need."

"That's me," he chirped.

Dolefully, I opened the front door and stepped inside. The house didn't feel right. It was cold. The heating had been turned off and the cluster of coats that normally smothered the banister at the bottom of the stairs had vanished.

I switched on the light and instantly realised that Andy was right. She'd gone. The living-room looked naked. Her knickknacks were missing, the walls were bare and the curtains had disappeared.

"Let's get pissed," said Andy. He pointed at a few bottles of booze in the corner, where the dark-wood cabinet used to be.

I was beginning to regret letting Andy into the house. I wanted some time, some private time, to process everything. "I wonder if I should have some time to myself."

"Charming. Some mate, you are. I could have been stopped by the police. Done for drink driving. But I didn't care. I just wanted to get my old pal back home safe."

"It's just that I…"

"You're embarrassed. I get it. I've been there. But I can help."

He was here for the night. He had that look. The one that meant business. Andy took drinking seriously. When the mood took him, nothing was going to stand in his way. Least of all, some pathetic mate's feelings.

"I'm not embarrassed," I quipped, "it's just that it might be better if…" But I knew he'd covered my arse that night. I didn't want to be totally ungrateful.

Andy read my expression. "So, you want me to fuck off?"

"I never said that."

"Look, mate," he pressed, "I stood where you're standing less than a year ago. I crumpled onto the carpet and wept like a baby. Go ahead. It's ok."

He stared at me for a moment, as if he was giving me permission.

"Anyway," he continued, obviously annoyed that I wasn't leaking all over the place, "we need to see what she's been up to, and with who. There's a good chance that there's a clue in this house. Something she's missed.

"Piss off, Andy."

Andy placed a brimming glass of bubbly into my hand and then switched on the TV, but there was no picture, just a mishmash of black and white dots accompanied by a loud hiss.

I peeled off my shoes and socks before slumping into the couch.

Andy shook his head remorsefully. "What a bitch. She's actually gone and nicked your satellite box. Now that, my son, is below the belt."

I suddenly got to my feet. "What else has she taken?"

The missing items were as follows: All her patterned dishes, our Italian hardwood double bed, a painting by a Sardinian artist called Corveche, (which I knew to be Maria's favourite) and about three quarters of our CDs. She'd left the Wishbone Ash albums and a copy of Cliff Richard–Live at the Palladium.

Every time I realised something was missing, Andy would punctuate the loss with the word 'bitch', the tone and emphasis varying, depending upon his perceived value of the item. When he found out she'd taken my Martin double 'O' acoustic, he actually offered to pay for a hit man.

It was then, as we checked behind the sofa for any stray music DVDs that may have evaded capture, that we noticed the large removal van parked across the street. It had the name 'Azuni', slap bang in the middle of some blobby outline, and a web address that ran the full length of the canvas flap– www.azunimove.it

"Is that always parked there?" asked Andy.

"Nope." I screwed up my eyes. "You don't think..."

"I do think," said Andy. "Maria's Italian, right?"

"Yeah, but..." My mind was spinning like a roulette wheel, and I didn't know where it was going to stop. "Is that an island on the side of the van?"

Andy spread his fingers on the window as he peered out into the street. "It looks a bit like Wales."

"Wales isn't a bloody island," I muttered.

"Well, it bloody should be," said Andy.

I remembered that his ex-wife, Wendy, was Welsh. As a result, the whole nation had been scrubbed from his Christmas list, forever.

Andy hesitated then hissed, "Get down. Now!"

Instinctively, I ducked down behind the sofa.

"There's someone in the cabin," whispered Andy. "It looked like a bloke."

I slid off the sofa and onto the carpet. "I should ask him what he's doing," I announced, still too nervous to stand up.

"He might be doing Maria right now," squeaked Andy. "Best not disturb them."

"Fuck off," I snapped.

Four sheets to the wind, Andy crawled commando-style to the edge of the sofa before lurching to his feet.

An ugly looking standard lamp, one of the few survivors of Maria's raid, toppled. Andy tried to save it and ended up doing a tango with the damn thing in full view of the mystery driver.

"Fuck! I think he's seen us," said Andy.

"You think?" I whispered sharply.

Slowly, we both stood up to find the driver of the van standing at the edge of my garden.

Andy hissed at me from the side of his mouth, "What do we

do now?"

I didn't know. "What does he want?" I hissed back.

"He's probably part removal-man, part assassin," said Andy, "I bet he's got a mission statement and everything. You know the kind of thing–'Removal's my game, but I'm criminally insane!', or 'Removals are painless, with Azuni, you're blameless', or–"

"Will you shut up!"

"Oh, no," wailed Andy, his eyes still fixed on the figure outside.

The driver had pushed my gate open. He was only a few yards from my front door.

The bell rang.

"Are you gonna answer it?" wheezed Andy.

"Of course I am." I straightened, folding my right hand into a fist.

Andy took a quick swig of bubbly then disappeared into the kitchen. "I'm off to get back up."

A blast of icy air hit me as my front door squeaked open.

"Mr Angus? Ian Angus?"

I nodded dumbly. The man had a strong Italian accent that reminded me of every Godfather film I'd ever seen. His face was pockmarked, pale and expressionless.

"Your wife asked me to make sure that you had received her letter and this." He handed me a parcel, then glanced over my shoulder at Andy skulking back from the kitchen, a deadly soup ladle in his hand.

"Your body guard?" asked the driver.

"Nah," I said, dismissively.

The driver smiled. It was the kind of smile someone makes before they commit cold, callous murder. "You see, I promised her I would give you that parcel in person."

The roulette wheel in my head was spun wildly.

CHAPTER FOUR

There was no sign of a gun or a knife. In fact, the mysterious driver had nothing more than a dangerous look in his eyes and a disarming smile. I'm not sure why, it might have been the brilliant whiteness of his teeth or the way he seemed to know so much about my predicament, but I decided to let him in.

As I backed into my own house like some subservient parishioner letting the vicar in for a cup of tea, I saw Andy drop his 'deadly' ladle and kick it out of reach. I half-expected him to whistle and stare at his nails.

The big Italian moseyed into the living-room and plumped himself down on my sofa beside the parcel I'd just put down and the crumpled letter I'd taken from my jacket. He beamed and tapped the envelope with a long spindly finger. "The letter first," he said, his voice firm.

"I've read it," I blurted.

"So have I," added Andy.

He glowered at Andy as if he'd just farted.

"Read it again," he ordered.

I began opening the letter with my nails, easing my forefinger under the remnants of the gummy seal.

There was a single sheet of lined paper inside.

I teased it free and read the first few lines in my head.

'Ian, it's over. What I have taken is all I want. No more. You can keep your pension and the house.'

I looked up to see Andy's inquisitive face barely a foot away from mine. "You knew she was gone," I whispered, staccato-style.

"I told you."

The big Italian shooed Andy away.

'The pact we made when we got engaged was endorsed by my family, so I am doubly committed to it. I'm going back home. Please don't try to follow me.'

The big Italian pointed to the parcel and Andy took another nervous slurp of bubbly.

I picked the parcel up and gave it a shake. I tore away the outer layer of brown paper until eventually found my way in and tipped the contents onto the sofa.

"Postcards," said Andy. He sounded deflated.

I undid the elastic band that held them together and began filtering through the pile. "They're all from Maria." I looked at the big Italian. "Is that it?"

He shrugged and stood up. "Just read them," he said, matter-of-factly.

I caught him before he reached the door. "All my stuff... Is it in the van?"

He paused on my front step and said, "No, Ian. All Maria's stuff is in the van." After another few paces he seemed to remember something.

Andy had pushed in beside me and we both teetered on the front door step. I felt the cold metal of the weather-bar on my bare feet.

The big Italian waved a finger of warning and said, "Do not try to follow me. Do not try to find Maria. You are dead to her."

My heart almost stopped there and then. I could hear Andy chittering with cold beside me.

"Or what?" added Andy in a drunken slur.

I stared at him in disbelief.

The big Italian stopped dead. He turned, narrowed his eyes and said, "Or I will kill you ..." he paused for a moment, as if savouring our fear. Using his forefinger and thumb to form an imaginary gun, he flicked his thumb down first at me and then at Andy. "... both."

In a pleading, pathetic voice, I said, "I don't understand."

Without moving position the big Italian gave us that smile again ... the one that meant business. "Ciao."

Too afraid to move, we watched him climb into his cab and start up the engine. The van, with the mystery island and the word 'Azuni' on the side, eased away from the halo of an orange street lamp and disappeared into the night.

"We should call the police," I said.

"And say what?" replied Andy.

"That we've been threatened." I thought about what Andy had told me earlier. "You said that Maria looked worried."

Andy slumped back down into the sofa. "I thought she did, but it might have been sadness or..."

"What if she was in the back of that van?" I blurted.

None of us said anything for a few seconds.

"Phone her," said Andy.

"She won't answer." I replied.

Andy took out his mobile and dialled.

"Why would you have her number?" I snapped.

"Because you're a dick and you never had your mobile with you when you played in the band," he snapped back.

I patted my pockets. He was right.

"See," he said, still listening. He suddenly stared down at the screen and swore.

"What is it?" I slurred.

He passed me the phone and I listened to a recording explaining that the number was now unobtainable.

I watched Andy stare out into the empty street. "She wasn't in the van. All this was planned. She's changed her number or something." He reached down for the postcards but I scooped them up before he could get them.

"I still think we should call the police," I said. My thoughts were cluttered.

"They'll just accuse you of bumping her off and bang you up," said Andy, as if it was the surest thing in the world.

"They will?" I mumbled.

"My brother was robbed at gunpoint and he had over twenty police visits, each more menacing than the last."

I wasn't sure where he was going with this.

"They pretty much decided that he deserved it because he was smoking dope at the time," explained Andy. "Just chill and tell me about that pact you made."

"It was stupid stuff," I moaned.

"Spit it out," he pressed, now drinking from a bottle of half-finished sherry.

"We said, when we got engaged, that marriage should only last a certain time."

"How long?"

"Ten years."

"I wish. Mine lasted two," moaned Andy. "And what was the

pact she made with her family?"

"I don't know," I said.

"Have you ever met her family?" asked Andy.

"No. Well, not apart from the wedding. Her dad had passed away and her mum was really ill." I paused for a moment. "Wasn't your mother Italian?"

"Till the day she died," said Andy. "Italian mum, Cockney dad." Andy started pointing at the TV. "Can you get internet on that thing?"

"Not without a box."

"Mmm..." Andy produced a USB stick and plugged it into the telly. "Your neighbour's Wi-Fi is unprotected."

He was always good at computer stuff.

"Where's your marriage certificate?"

"I don't fucking know." I was in no mood for Andy's shit. It was almost three in the morning.

He found the Google search engine on the TV and typed in the words 'Italian islands'. Immediately, a selection of maps covered the screen.

I pointed to one shaped a bit like Wales. "It's Sardinia."

"That's what it says." He turned to me—then dropped the bottle of sherry on the carpet.

'For fuck's sake, Andy." I rushed to get a cloth.

"Ever been?" he shouted after me.

"Of course I have," I answered, "That's where we met. It's where Maria comes from."

"Well, why didn't you say so before?"

"I don't know."

I began scrubbing the carpet.

"You really are a self-centred ass," he continued. I've known you for years and you never once said where your wife came from."

"Why would I?"

Andy just shook his head. "So, Maria has gone back to her real home, Sardinia?"

"That's what it says in the letter," I sighed.

"What's her second name, again?"

"I could never pronounce it right," I said. "Savian... Maria Saviano."

Andy began typing: 'Mafia gangs of Sardinia'.

"What the hell?" I gasped.

"Wait a minute," warned Andy, all animated and flushed with booze. "The results are pretty sketchy. The article says that the main Mafia families are in based four regions of Italy: Campania, Calabria, Sicily and Puglia.

"No mention of Sardinia," I said.

Andy added the surname, 'Saviano' to another search and waited.

There were two results. The first referred to an olive oil exporter; the second, Andy read it out with gusto, "Saviano, once of Sicily, was forced to flee to Sardinia after he was reportedly involved, along with a rival family, the Galdinis, in the murder of four judges."

"This is crazy," I protested.

"Get this..." Andy continued, "although there was no hard evidence to connect him with the Sicilian hits, he was arrested by the Italian police on two separate counts of money laundering and fraud." He pointed at the letter then looked straight at me. "He was sentenced to ten years."

"Absolute crap," I said, taking the bottle from him before he dropped it again. "The internet can spout out any old shit. There is nothing to link my Maria with this gangster."

Andy continued to read down the page. "Shit," he gasped.

"What now?" I moaned.

"What was Maria's dad's name?" He pressed.

"I have no idea."

"Okay," said Andy, "let me put it another way. What was your dog's name."

"Fuck off, Andy."

"Charlie, right?" pressed Andy. He flicked down the web page and zoomed in on a blurred black and white picture of a young mobster called, Charles Saviano.

"And?"

"And you don't need to be a fuckin' rocket scientist to work it out. She even looks like him. Maria is the daughter of a Mafia boss called Charles Saviano, and guess what?"

I shuddered to think.

"And he got out of jail last month."

CHAPTER FIVE

It was ten in the morning when I heard the phone buzz into life. My head was aching like a bastard, and there was someone sleeping next to me… with their arm around me.

"Andy! Bugger off!"

Andy woke up with a jolt and I watched him shuffle out of bed. He flicked his hands, like he'd just dipped his fingernails in a bucket of shit. "Yuck!"

"Put it away." I pointed. Andy, much skinnier than me, had pulled a pair of my pyjamas on and forgot to button them up. I made for the stairs and shouted over my shoulder, "That's put me right off my cornflakes, that has."

Andy laughed and let one rip.

"Piss off home to your own house, you dirty bastard. No wonder Wendy buggered off." I staggered down the last few steps just as the phone stopped buzzing. I stared at the white receiver for a minute as if it might jump back to life. It didn't, so I swore and, on autopilot, slipped into the downstairs toilet and began brushing my teeth. I thought back to the horrors of the previous day. "Jesus!" I stopped and squinted into the mirror, a pink toothbrush dangling from the side of my mouth like a second tongue. My hair was a mess but my eye hadn't blackened as predicted.

"I've got a plan," announced Andy.

"So have I," I blurted, my mouth still full of toothpaste. "You're going home."

"Now, wait a minute," said Andy, "who rescued you from the American with no neck?" He pointed at my eye and looked disappointed. "No shiner?"

This was all happening too quickly. "I…"

"Who drove you home?" He persisted.

I was struggling. "But…"

"And who found out that you were married to the mob?"

Both hands on the rim of the sink, I let the toothbrush fall from my mouth and clatter into the sink.

I plodded back to the phone and pressed 147. The phone rang twice and then said, "Number unobtainable."

Andy appeared in the doorway of the kitchen holding a single silver spoon. "She's left you fuck all. There's nothing to turn the bacon with. She's half-inched the fish slice. It was her mum's or something."

I handed him the ladle he'd dropped in the living-room the night before. "There!"

"Anyway," he continued, "I have a plan."

"You said. But before you tell me this wonderful plan, how did you end up in my bed?"

"Ah," said Andy, trying, in vain, to scoop a rind of bacon out from the edge of the frying pan, "the sofa has a lump in it. It was digging into my back."

I sat down at our scratched pine table and looked out of the patio doors, across the valley. It was early April, and the birch trees at the bottom of our garden swished their silver-green leaves in the breeze.

Andy pushed a bacon sandwich towards me and sat down with his. "The way I see it, you're a free agent now."

I was going to put him right, but I had a mouthful of bacon and he took advantage.

"You don't have a wife to nag you any more, and..." He took another massive bite of his butty. "I'm looking for a guitarist-come-singer for a month's work around the Med."

I looked at him incredulously. "Does your plan include me going to Sardinia to try and rescue my wife, by any chance?"

He issued a pained sigh and said, "It might do? But only if you were insane," he added. "Why would I want to get mixed up with the Italian Mafia? Maria's a lost cause. Let her go back to her killer dad and nurse him, or whatever she's gonna do. Maybe she's supposed to take over the family business out there. Who knows?"

"She might be in trouble," I said.

"There is no 'might' about it, pal. So, let it go." He stood up and took my empty plate over to the sink. "Besides, we gave that nice Azuni man our word that we wouldn't follow him."

"Bollocks. You stood with your mouth open, scared shitless,

just like me. We both watched him walk off," I reminded him.

"That still counts as a promise in my book," said Andy.

It was then that I remembered the key—the brass key that Maria had slipped from her neck-chain in the restaurant.

"Where are you going?" asked Andy.

I popped into the hall and returned with the key, the letter and the pile of postcards, which I arranged neatly on the kitchen table.

"What's the key all about?" asked Andy.

"Good question," I replied. "We got this key on 'Dead Dog Beach'."

"Where?"

"It's the place where I proposed," I explained.

"What kind of name is that?"

"It was our name. Our special name for that place."

"Why?"

"Well, we were sunbathing on a beach one day when something pretty horrible happened. The place was packed, and the sea was as blue as it gets. We were just about to go for a swim when a kid called out and pointed at something in the water.

Of course, the first thing that came into my mind was a shark or some other kid in trouble, but it was neither of those things."

"What was it?" said Andy. He pulled a lump of rind away from the bacon in his sandwich and dangled it like a worm above his mouth before dropping it in.

I watched him chomp as I explained, "More and more children began pointing at a spot in sea, about a hundred yards out. It looked like someone was floating, face down, in the water. Their hair was splayed out around their head, their arms stretched out in front of them like this." I demonstrated. "The closer the corpse drifted in towards the beach, the more and more people retreated out of the water. Mums and dads began pulling their kids up the sand, away from the shore. Just like that bit in 'Jaws' where they all race out of the water. There was a mad panic that ended with the everyone standing about ten feet from the water's edge. We couldn't believe it."

"I could," said Andy, "you were deep in fuckin' Mafia country."

"Anyway," I continued, "the stalemate was eventually broken

by an old man, who must have been eighty-odds. He was distraught and he waded straight into the sea and caught hold of the corpse. I swear, the whole beach seemed to gasp at once. He grabbed it by the hair and pulled it into the shallows. It was then that Maria let go of my hand and waded out to help him."

"Why?"

"There were hundreds of people there and yet she was the only one, apart from the old man, with enough guts to go in."

"Fuckin' hell," Andy whispered.

"Anyway, when she reached the corpse, I could see that the old man was crying."

"What?"

"Maria and the old man said something in Italian to each other, then lifted the corpse free of the water."

"And?"

"And it was a dog. A dead dog."

"Yuck."

"Yeah. So, they lifted the poor thing all the way up the beach, through a gauntlet of onlookers, to the dunes, where the old man buried it."

"Why was he crying?"

"It was his fuckin dog," I answered. "We called that place *Dead Dog Beach* from then on. Funny thing was, no one went back into the sea that day. I always thought that was weird because the sea must be full of dead things. Yet I felt the same. The dead dog had put me off going back in too."

"So this is relevant because?" pressed Andy.

"It's totally relevant because the old man came up to Maria as we were leaving the beach. He didn't look well."

"He wouldn't. His dog had just died."

"Yes, but then he began coughing and clutching his chest."

"Jesus. Then what?"

"Then he died," I finished. I pointed to the brass key that lay on my kitchen table. "But before he did, he gave that key to Maria. She said he took from the dog's collar."

"Why did he give it to her?" asked Andy.

"I've never been sure. I suppose it was to say thanks for helping him when no one else would."

"So, how did the dog get in the sea in the first place? Where did it come from?" asked Andy.

I shrugged. "All I know is that I asked her to marry me the same day, and that she wore that key around her neck for ten years, like a charm, until yesterday evening."

"So what's her game, Ian? What is she hiding? Where has she really gone?"

"That's what I need to find out," I said, having no clue where to begin.

"Shit," said Andy. "We're going to Sardinia, aren't we?"

"I have to find out for sure."

"You see, I had a different plan," he said.

"I bet. Your plan was to play gigs around the Med, get drunk and chase women. Right?"

Andy sighed. "Shit, shit and triple shit. I know the agent that's organising a whole bunch of foreign gigs. He told me to say where and he would fix something. We'll have first dibs." Andy went into the living-room and switched on the interactive TV. "Look," he said, pointing to a series of red dots in and around Italy. "There are two resorts on Sardinia–one in Calgliari and one in Bosa. I could ask about Sardinia. Go for a month and, at the same time, find out what she's up to."

"But Azuni said he would kill us if we followed him?" I reminded him.

"We'll need a bass player. It has to be a live band, no backing tapes," continued Andy.

"There's no such thing as tapes any more, dick head." There probably was, but everything was MP3's and WAV files these days.

"What about Mad Willie Marvin?" said Andy, a wry look on his face.

"No way," I said, "do you really want a bass player that jumps up on pub tables, picks fights with the bar staff, and shags anything that moves?"

Andy opened his hands and gave me one of his stupid, quizzical pouts. "Sounds perfect."

CHAPTER SIX

An empty house and a neighbour that worked on the rigs meant that we could set up and rehearse in my living room. Andy's drum kit was outside in the van but Willie had to lug his Ampeg rig here in a taxi and set up.

Willie, tall and pale, always sporting a hang dog expression, nodded a kind of reluctant hello and murmured, "Sardinia, eh?"

"Why not?" chirped Andy. "It's not as if any of us have got anything better to do."

Willie looked Andy straight in the eye and pointed at me. "The only reason I'm in is cos I need some cash. Keep that prick away from me."

The old wounds were still there. Willie reckoned he had helped write the one song that ever made me any money. He hadn't. It was all in the can. All he did was play bass on the demo. I could see Andy shaking his head.

"We need to let that boat sail, Willie." Andy glanced over at me.

Willie was still growling. "He fuckin' owes us."

"The way I see it, we owe him. He's been slagged off for years for that shit song."

Willie grunted, then hauled his rig into position in front of the living room window. The room was suddenly much darker.

"He's the same as us now," continued Andy. "He's waiting for 'that call', the one that will never come."

Andy was right. Things had stopped dead for me a long time ago. We were all occasional musicians … In my case, I'd done nothing for the last eight years. Cadgers, bums, on-the-dole-off-the-dole layabouts who used the system any way they could to maintain a state of readiness for a day that would never come. I thought about 'that call' nearly every day—*"Okay, Ian, we want to offer you a five-album deal. You'll need to go back out on tour – and we'll have to sort out all the royalties you're owed …"* This crazy trip was probably as close as I'd ever to get to 'that call' now.

"Can you bury the hatchet, Willie?" I asked. It was a perfectly reasonable question, I thought. But you could never tell with Mad Willie Marvin.

He glowered at me with his beady, black eyes. It wasn't always easy to see his eyes because they were screened off by an unruly mop of red hair, but I caught enough of a glimpse to know that he was pissed off. "Only if it's in your head, ye fanny," he replied.

"Ok," I replied, already testing the weight of my Gibson Les Paul. It hung heavy around my neck that day. I hadn't picked it up for about a month and had forgotten what a bastard it was. Great sound, great feel, but a ton weight.

Willie blew out the side of his mouth and his ginger mop lifted like the edge of a curtain. "Andy's the man with the plan, the one in charge, not you. Ok?"

I shrugged.

Andy gave a 'thumbs up', then thumped on the bass drum a few more times. "We can get all the way there in my Transit van. I worked it out on my route planner. It's about one thousand five-hundred miles. We can either go to the south coast, over to France, and straight down to Marseille, or we can go the scenic route, through Switzerland and Northern Italy?"

"We'll need a gig every night to pay for fuel and digs," I reminded him.

Willie adjusted the tone of his amp. "Pay your own fuel and digs. I better get a wage every night."

I'd forgotten what a tight-wad he was. Willie could peel an orange in his pocket.

"I'll sort all that out," said Andy.

"I'm only doing this for one reason," I said.

"We know," said Willie, "love."

I bristled. "Not necessarily. She might be in danger."

Willie stopped tuning his Fender Precision and flicked his ginger comb-over out of his eyes again. "Don't talk pish. If you were that worried about her, you would have called the police. She went of her own accord, all planned and everything. Andy told me the whole fuckin' thing."

I stared at Andy, who ducked down behind a cymbal and pretended to tighten his snare. "Thanks, Pal," I muttered.

"Anyway," continued Willie, "you're better off without her.

You've never been a free man in your whole life."

Willie was right. I'd met Maria when I was twenty. Before that I'd gone out with Debbie Davidson for three years. I was pretty horrible to Debbie. Always rehearsing, drinking with the band and playing gigs, I didn't really pay her enough attention. She buggered off with Alex McGraw, the brain-box of Milton High. I can't blame her. But even with Debbie, I never strayed once. Willie had a whole lot more experience than I'd ever had, and Andy wasn't far behind him.

"I'll get my agent to line up some gigs en route," said Andy, chirpily changing the subject."

"What fuckin' agent?" barked Willie.

Andy tapped the side of his nose.

I gave the P.A. the customary, "One, two... One, two."

I looked over at the two of them, waiting to see what I was going to say. "Let's try *Wishin' Well.*"

Andy counted us in.

It sounded pretty good up to the last guitar solo, where I hit a few bum notes. I finished with a '*Who*-like, wind-milling double crescendo in A minor'.

"Nice," said Andy.

"Apart from your fuck up in the solo," added Willie. He grinned at me and shook his head, like I was some kind of rookie. How come a great big star like you can fuck up like that, eh?"

"Shut up, Willie." He wasn't going to let it go.

"The Eurovision Song Contest would have kicked you and your song into touch if you'd played like that."

"Yeah, let's play *Bling Blang Bong,*" chirped Andy.

"Ha, ha," I replied, sarcastically. Now, B*ling, Blang Bong* wasn't exactly a rock classic, but it had reached Number 15 in the French charts, been played on about fifty TV shows—and there had been a European tour on the back of it. A whole lot more than these two gits had ever done and they knew it. Andy was fine with it, but Willie was still very bitter.

Willie eyed me through his hair. "Was there two chords or three chords in that song?"

"Give it a rest, Willie."

I could have said a lot worse but I held back. I needed this nutcase for the time being. Unlike me, Willie was always up for a fight.

Andy thumped out the beginning of Queen's 'We Will Rock You'.

I thought of Azuni and his threat. I thought of Maria and wondered what she was doing right now. Was she missing me, or was she back where she belonged?

"Numb nuts!" snapped Willie, "Sing it!"

I eased towards the mic and gripped it with both hands.

* * *

Three hours later, it was just Andy and myself sitting at my kitchen table again. He'd practically moved in.

"Why did you have to tell Willie everything?" I said.

Andy shrugged. "I thought he deserved to know what he was getting into."

"So what did you say?"

Andy cracked open a can of lager. "I told him that your missus is mixed up with the Mafia, and you want to check if she's alright."

My mouth dropped open in disbelief. "Why?"

Andy took a long swig of his beer, "because that's the truth, isn't it?"

"Not really," I said. "I want to see if we're doing the right thing by splitting up. All that Mafia shit is in your head. We don't have any real proof."

Well," said Andy, his face full of mischief. "I had a look at those postcards last night, and I–"

"You did what?" I opened the bread bin and saw that it was empty.

"I mean," continued Andy, "who planks anything in a bread bin and expects it to stay hidden. "Every time I had a jam sandwich, they were staring at me, taunting me. A little voice in my head said, 'Andy, have a look... read the postcards... use them to help Ian'."

"You really are a complete 'Dick', aren't you?" I caught him by the collar, ready to smack him one. "That's my private stuff!"

But he just winked at me and said, "They're in chronological order." He brushed my hand away.

I narrowed my eyes and tried to stare him out.

"They're snapshots of how she felt about you. They were all sent to that pal of hers – Julie Grant. The one that got killed in that car crash up on the by-pass."

"I know how Maria felt about me," I snapped.

"You knew fuck all," he said, all sinister and mightier than thou.

"What do you mean?" I pressed.

"Before I tell you what I mean, I'm going to tell you what I think."

I wanted Andy out of my house. "I don't suppose I've got any choice, eh?"

"Not really," he quipped.

I made to grab him again, but he put his hand up to stop me.

"You haven't even bothered to look at them, have you?"

"Not yet, but..."

Andy tapped his temple, woodpecker-style, with his right forefinger. "That in itself speaks volumes my friend, fuckin' volumes."

I closed my eyes and tried to calm down. "So what are you saying?"

"I'm saying that you should give it a try."

"Give what a try?"

"Let me use the cards to help you see things the way Maria saw them. See the world from her perspective."

"You? Steady Eddie? The man who never stopped playing around in or out of marriage? You, the man who's never held down a job or a promise his whole life?"

"Don't start," barked Andy. "You cadged off Maria for ten years. Poncing about like you were Jimmy Page after your big one hit wonder."

"Look, Andy, just because I didn't take you or Willie on that tour didn't mean I didn't like you as players or friends. It was a management decision."

Andy gave me a sly smile. "So was your marriage, if you ask me."

"What the fuck are you on about?"

"Sit back and I'll enlighten you." He waved the bundle of cards in my face.

I threw my hands up in defeat. "Fine, do your thing. I suppose you want me to lie down on the couch?"

"Now that would be pervy," said Andy, "No, just let me take you back," he said, producing the first battered-looking postcard. "There are only six cards dating back to two thousand and eight. The first one is pretty up beat. You'd been to Marseille on your first holiday. Maria was still home-sick. You went all the way there—"

"We went all the way there on the train," I finished. I remembered the double cabin, the excitement of our first trip as a married couple. I'm almost certain we got the whole holiday for about a hundred quid each.

"And I quote," began Andy, *Ian is so careful around me. He handles me like an unexploded bomb. But then I had a tummy upset and he automatically decided I was pregnant. He told me that I couldn't go in the sea, or the pool, or eat brie. There's no way he's ever going to tell me what I can and can't do. I decided that he wants to control me rather than love me. I've also noticed that he's very jealous. He keeps interrupting waiters whenever they start talking to me, or showing any interest. He's so immature. Still, the weather is beautiful and I've stopped feeling so sic– homesick, that is. I do, however, have an unquenchable desire for liquorice. I hope he's not right about being pregnant. Wish you were here, Julie–with a big bag of liquorice. Xx Maria.*"

"She said I was jealous?"

Andy gave me a tight-lipped smile. "And a controlling bastard. Only natural, I would have said. She was hot. Still is," he added.

Maria was a dark-skinned beauty, a catch in a million. I had been so lucky to find her, to have her say 'Yes' to me.

"She was always too good for you," murmured Andy, as if reading my mind.

"So, I should just thank my lucky stars for the time I had with her and bow out?"

He shrugged. "I'm just saying–it seems like you knew what you had back then, mate." He waved the postcard as if he was drying a Polaroid.

I snatched it from him and stared at the picture. It showed the Place Castellane, an ornate fountain with a Nelson's column-type structure protruding from the centre of a big roundabout. I slowly looked up at him and said, "What did you mean about our marriage being a management decision?"

Andy was just about to answer when his mobile rang.

He stared down at the screen and nodded. "My agent's come good again. We're going to Sardinia via France. He's even got us a gig in Dover the night before the ferry crossing to Calais."

"That was quick," I mumbled. My head was still thumping. Why did Maria really leave me these postcards? And who was the big Italian who made sure I got them?

CHAPTER SEVEN

I hate motorway service stations. I hate how everything is twice the price it should be and twice as crap. I bought a chicken wrap which disintegrated as soon as we got back in the van. "Shit!" One bite and a squirt of chilli paste and chicken burst out of the opposite end like an exploding cigar—all over my jeans.

Andy erupted. "You stupid git. You should have got a Macky-dee's like us." He offered me a long, limp chip, his whole body still shaking with laughter.

"Piss off," I muttered, flicking the gunge off my legs.

I sat next to Willie who had a McChicken Sandwich in one hand and a large Coke in the other. He hit the accelerator and steered us into the middle lane with his knees. The old double-wheelbase, Ford Transit rattled like a bastard when it hit fifty and then evened out around sixty-five. It had been a long day driving down the motorway, pointless rows of cones and average speed cameras keeping us in check all the way.

"Where are we now?" I asked, dabbing my jeans with a paper hanky.

"We're about fifty miles from Dover," said Willie. "What's this place we're at tonight, Andy?"

Andy stuffed the last of his chips into his mouth and chucked the empty red and yellow carton into the foot-well. "It's ... it's called 'The ... Pit'."

"Sounds lovely," I mumbled.

"They're paying three hundred for a two-hour set," said Andy. "Says here," he squinted at his phone as we bumped onto a B road with high hedges on either side, "that it's above the harbour, on Castle Road. You want to be on the A258." Andy switched to another app on his phone. "They want a soul set."

Willie hit the brakes and pulled into a lay-by.

We both stared at Andy.

"I said it would be no problem," he said, mostly to himself.

"We don't know any soul stuff," growled Willie.

"Well, we'll just have to soul it up a bit. Take what we've got and add a pinch of soul," said Andy.

"How the fuck do you add a pinch of soul to '*Sweet Child of Mine*'?" asked Willie.

"Look, Ian, you used to do the weddings the same as me. It's easy. Tell him."

"Easy for a drummer," I replied, "I need to learn lyrics and chords, and shit."

Andy cut in. "But you still remember stuff from playing those weddings, don't you?"

"No, I don't." I thought about this all the way to Castle Road and managed to prove myself wrong by remembering *Let's Stick Together*, a Motown medley, *Everlasting Love* and *Soul Man*. Once we reached the venue, Andy got busy downloading lyrics and chords from the internet, while Willie and myself set up.

The Pit was exactly 'what it said on the tin'. The stage had been taped together with grey tape, while the bar was dimly lit and sparsely populated. The choices were either cider, beer or shots. The dance floor was a sticky mess, and the chairs, at least what was left of them, were covered in damp, burgundy velvet that stunk of B.O. and disinfectant.

"Nice," I said, as I adjusted my mic stand.

"We've played worse," said Willie. He tapped his own mic and said, "Three beers for the band." It boomed out over the two-thousand-watt P.A.

The barman, a fat guy in his fifties, looked up and gave him the finger.

"Naw," said Willie, "three, ya wank!"

I cupped my mic. "Willie! For Christ sake."

The fat barman looked at us side-on, as if he was trying to work out if Willie was kidding or not.

I beamed at him and gave him the thumbs up, which seemed to work as he began cleaning glasses again.

"I guess it's gonna have to be self-service," said Willie.

"Willie, don't go stealing stuff," snapped Andy, "We might need to play here again on the way back."

"They deserve it," he reasoned. He plugged his bass into his rig and thumped out the beginning to 'Another One Bites the Dust'.

A few locals filtered in and gave him 'the finger'.

"This is gonna be a ball, I can just tell," I groaned.

Andy jumped on stage to tweak his drums. We'd stuck them in position, but he still needed to tighten his snare and adjust his ride cymbal. "Here," he said, handing me a pile of paper. "That's as much as I could be arsed writing out."

I looked at the lyrics for a few minutes, flicking through the various tunes. "There are ten songs here and we need to play for two hours."

"The guy at the bar says they don't dance much anyway. They just come here to smoke dope and get wrecked." Andy waved a white envelope in our faces. "Paid up front. I told them we had to make a sharp exit."

The pressure was off. "We'll play a mix of rock and soul."

"Yeah. Fuck them," said Willie.

I looked at Andy and said, "Is that it? Aren't you going to put any stage clothes on, or …?"

"See!" said Willie, nodding at me, as if I was a total reject, "I told you he was a ponce."

Andy pointed to the gathering audience. "Do you really think that bunch would appreciate me slipping a silver, lamé leotard on?"

I scanned the bedraggled group of kids that had trundled past the stage. They looked as though they'd just been sentenced to fifty years' hard labour. "Not exactly a cheery bunch," I murmured, suddenly feeling overdressed in my pressed satin shirt.

Andy began surveying the room too, as it filled up. I knew exactly what he was thinking. Who were the best-looking girls? Were they alone or not? Who had the biggest tits, the best ass, the shortest skirt... He would typically compare notes with Willie during songs. I would be singing my lungs out and sweating as I tried to remember lyrics and chords, and they would be lining up women.

I'd seen it a hundred times. They had a code when they both homed in on a girl. A double nod meant they would ride her, and a double shake of the head meant 'no chance'. Most of the time they lived in fantasy land.

I always think it's a bastard when no one dances. Without a cluster of humans to soak up our songs and dampen our sound system, the music echoed round a dance floor like a nuclear explosion. Tonight was no exception, so we got the usual 'turn it down' signals from the bar staff. A few songs in and already a kind of 'us and them' mentality was building, especially with Willie. He was mouthing things like–'fuck them,' 'turn it up,' 'blow them off their seats'...

So, now I had to remember everything *and* keep him from starting World War Three.

At the break, we wandered over to the bar and a girl who'd been given the official double shake of rejection by the boys came over to talk to me.

"You from Scotland then?" she said.

I gave her a polite smile and nodded, turning back to my drink.

"So are you gonna dance or what?" she persisted.

Andy and Willie loved this kind of situation. To them, it was manna from heaven. Something to regurgitate endlessly whenever I got too cocky.

"I'm really tired, hen," I said.

She smiled coyly and asked, "Or do you just want to go round the back?"

"She's a trier, I'll give her that," said Andy, louder than he should have.

The girl drew Andy daggers before grabbing hold of my wrist.

"Go on, Ian," said Willie, "you're a free man." He gave the girl a wink and she pulled me out onto the dance floor.

She was too tall and skinny for my liking, with a chin sharp enough to cut glass. It almost had my eye out as she spun me round.

Andy and Willie were in hysterics as she gyrated and bobbed up and down while I daddy danced like a complete wanker, shuffling from one foot to the other, fists bobbing at my chest.

The song playing was, 'Do You Think I'm Sexy', by Rod Stewart. It's a song where you could at least keep a safe distance away from your partner. But then Andy said something to the barman and the music changed. The whole place soon oozed sex as the first few bars of 'Let's Get it On' filled the room. This was a song designed for close, intimate contact.

"Bastards," I mouthed, but I doubt they heard me or saw me,

because they were both doubled up. I was locked in a jagged cage of arms and legs, a hungry, searching mouth trying to latch onto mine.

"My name is Cherrie," she yelled, over the music.

I pointed to the guys. "I better get back to my..." But it was too late, her lips had welded themselves onto mine, a slippery tongue that tasted of garlic and fags already probing around like a snooping snake.

It wouldn't have been so awful if we'd been buried, six deep, in an impenetrable crowd of dancers, but we weren't; we were alone on a vast dance floor, surrounded by about a hundred cheering onlookers.

Even the fat barman looked like he was in tears, laughing his head off.

"The Stripper!" shouted Andy. I could hear him screaming at the barman like a girl above the dulcet tones of Marvin. "I'm begging you, put on the Stripper!"

It was now or never, so as the first pangs of 'da ra da da' echoed over The Pit's grimy dance floor, I ducked out from the clutches of the stick insect and bolted like the true coward I was. I ran to the back of the stage and almost smashed into another girl. "Sorry," I blurted.

"You dance good," she said.

I couldn't really see her. It was dark, but she had an accent. I think it was French. "I ..." I pointed back to the dance-floor. "I didn't really want to ..." But the mysterious girl had gone.

An hour-and-a-half later, Andy and Willie were still in stitches. They loaded up the van as I walked back and forward through the gauntlet of wild Dover Kids. Each time I tried to squeeze passed them with a huge speaker and said, "Eh, excuse me," or "Coming through," they ignored me. It was as if the Men in Black had erased their memories. They were always IN THE FUCKING WAY!

As we drove down to the harbour, I had to suffer the sound of Willie and Andy giving me their best rendition of 'Let's Get It On' by Marvin, fucking Gaye!

CHAPTER EIGHT

Willie could sleep anywhere. In the van, on stage, in his guitar case, even here—on a busy ferry.

Andy and I, on the other hand, were still buzzing after the gig. We had too much to catch up on.

"Has Maria contacted you yet?" he said.

"Nope. I've tried calling her but that number is no good any more."

I looked across at Willie, stretched out on the floor of the lounge, sleeping soundly. He'd never been married. He used to tell me how he'd looked after his mum for years. Got some kind of carer allowance to do it as well. It couldn't have been much, as they lived in the shittiest part of the council estate. Endle Lane was mostly boarded up and off limits to all, including the police. I don't think I'd ever seen him wear anything else apart from jeans and a t-shirt, even when it was pissing down. He had a reputation though. He'd half-killed a burglar that had tried to rob his house. It was the middle of the night and, still naked, Willie had chased him up the street and then beat the crap out of him with a metal fence-paling. I never saw it in the papers, but everyone knew why Jonnie Muir was in a wheelchair. To be fair, Willie had only done what everyone else had wanted to do. Jonnie had been preying on the neighbourhood for years.

On the ferry, a group of men in the corner of the bar were laughing loudly.

"Does that guy with the Juventus scarf remind you of anyone?" Andy asked.

"How do you know it isn't a Newcastle scarf?" I said. "It's black and white too." The man wearing it, however, did look familiar.

"It has a dancing bull on it," said Andy. "When did you last see a dancing bull in Newcastle?"

"Well," I began.

"It's Juventus, trust me." Andy sipped his pint and narrowed his eyes. "Are you sure it isn't that freak with the big removal van, Azuni?"

"What? The one that said he would kill us if we followed Maria?"

"Yeah," Andy answered, absentmindedly.

"I fuckin' hope not." I said, looking closer.

The man turned to face me. A moment ago, he'd been laughing with his friends, but now his expression had turned stern. He sipped on his beer and continued to stare back at me.

I lowered my gaze just as a familiar voice said, "What's that twat looking at?"

Willie had woken up at the wrong time.

"It's nothing, Willie," I reassured. "We just thought it was someone we knew, but it's not. I'm sure of it."

But Willie got up to his feet and wandered straight over to the group of Juventus supporters. We could see now that they all wore the same black and white scarfs.

"I don't know why they're laughing, they should be pissed off," said Andy. He pointed at an abandoned newspaper which confirmed the result on its back page. Chelsea 2–Juventus 1.

"Willie," I whispered sharply.

"I'll go and get him," said Andy.

The boat was beginning to pitch and my stomach didn't feel good.

By now, I was convinced that the laughing group of Juventus fans were actually a band of Mafia hit men.

Willie went straight up to the one we thought looked like Azuni and prodded him on the chest with a long freckled finger. "Got a fuckin' problem, Pal?" he said.

One of the fans reached for the inside pocket of his jacket, but the Azuni lookalike grabbed his hand and shook his head. He turned to Willie, "No, I don't have a problem," said the man, in stilted English, "but you gonna have one if you doesn't back off right now."

One of the fans grabbed Willie's arm, but Willie, still maintaining his threatening gaze, caught the fan's wrist and twisted it back on itself with such force that the fan dropped to his knees with yelp.

Willie smiled. "What did you say?"

Another fan lashed out at Willie but he too dropped to the ground, blood jetting from his burst nose. Willie grabbed the Azuni lookalike and would have cracked him one too but a girl, seemingly oblivious to the stramash walked straight through the mêlée and up to the bar. People parted like she was royalty or something.

The fan who had reached for his inside pocket earlier did the same again, but this time he looked confused, patting his jacket as if something was missing.

Willie kicked him in the balls, then delivered a 'Glasgow kiss' to the Azuni lookalike.

The big Italian staggered back, dazed while the fan who'd reached for his pocket was clutching his nachos, like they'd become detached and had every chance of rolling out the bottom of his trousers.

Although the majority of the punters on the ferry didn't really see much, the barman had spotted that something was wrong and had called for help. Two hefty stewards were walking towards us.

Andy got to Willie just before he turned on the ferry staff. "It's nothing to worry about, guys," he assured, barring their way. He ushered Willie to one side, stared accusingly at the Juventus fans and said, "I'm sure that none of us want to spend the rest of the crossing in the hold, now do we?"

The Juventus fans began shouting in Italian.

"See," said Andy, addressing the stewards, "that's what they were like, before you arrived. Drunk and abusive." He pointed to Willie. "If it wasn't for my friend here, they'd have wrecked the place. That one," he singled out the one clutching his balls, "had his knob out. Mums and kids everywhere. It's just not on. I mean, I know they lost a match and stuff, but enough is enough."

I'd seen Andy in action before. A motor-mouthed cockney, he had a knack of flipping situations to his advantage. In this case, he used a lack of English on their part, a dash of 'us and them'. Of course, the 'paedo' trump card was sheer genius.

It worked beautifully. Within moments, three more staff members had joined in, and the original two began parroting Andy's version of events– adding a few embellishments of their own.

As the enraged ferry staff manhandled the wailing Italians

from the ship's bar, Willie and Andy began to clap. It was one of the best mass hypnotism shows I'd ever seen. Paul McKenna eat your heart out. The whole bar started clapping along, even though I'm pretty sure most of them had missed Willie's martial arts display. I watched them taunt the Italians as they were dragged through the busy lounge.

"Keelhaul them!" a drunk shouted from the corner.

CHAPTER NINE

I'd dozed off but when I woke Maria's brass key was beginning to bug me. Was it a token of our love, our marriage, or was there something I was missing? Maria handing it back to me at our disastrous dinner was probably nothing more than a symbolic gesture, the final nail in our marital coffin. Yet I'd often wondered what it was for. Why would a dog have a key round its neck other than as a trinket to engrave its name on? I guess it could have been an actual key to let it in and out of somewhere, or it was around the dog's neck because the mutt's owner didn't want to keep in an obvious place? Was it a special key that opened something important?

"Are you awake?" whispered Andy.

"Just," I moaned, yawning so hard I almost broke my jaw. "Argh." It was light outside. I could see Calais in the distance.

"Where's Willie?" asked Andy.

I saw that Willie had left his bass guitar by his empty seat.

Andy noticed too. "That's not like him."

It wasn't. I suddenly sat up and said, "The Italians."

"Nah," said Andy, "they're in the purser's office."

Still, I wondered if the Italians had somehow escaped the clutches of the purser and reaped revenge on Willie while we were sleeping.

Andy swung his feet off the seat and I followed suit. My foot clipped Willie's guitar case and I noticed something. "Why did he do that?" I asked, pointing at the words stencilled on the side. "Los Hombres?"

"It's the name of our new band," said Andy, all chuffed with himself.

"Let me guess," I said, "you think it sounds Italian?"

Andy gave me one of his stupid grins. "Exactly."

I tapped the case and said, "That's fuckin' Spanish, you eejit."

Andy's grin collapsed in on itself. "You sure?"

"Your mum was Italian!"

"She only ever spoke English to us," he muttered.

I gave him an incredulous look.

"Bastard," he moaned. "I made the stencil and everything."

"Where the fuck is Willie?" I asked this time.

"Let's hope he's not at the bottom of the Channel, wearing a pair of concrete boots," said Andy, heading for the toilets.

I followed, deciding the guitar would be safe enough for a few minutes. "He's probably having an 'Eartha Kitt'," I whispered, tiptoeing through a cluster of sleeping passengers.

Andy opened the door to the 'Gents' just as a very flustered lady staggered out past us. Dressed almost completely in black, she avoided eye contact with both of us and waddled off in the opposite direction.

I'd spotted a pair of red knickers hanging out of her handbag.

We waited a few moments until she turned the corner. I wasn't really sure whether she was a 'double shake' or a 'double wink'. Then the door of the Gents squeaked open again.

"Willie?" I yelped.

"Shit!" he yelped back.

"Somehow," said Andy, "I don't think that's what you were doing in there."

Willie flushed bright red.

Andy and I glanced at each other and gave a double wink at the same time.

"Mind your own business," snapped Willie.

We watched him shuffle over to his guitar case, his ginger mop ruffled, his face the colour of a baboon's arse. He stopped short of his seat turned back to face us. He pointed down at his guitar. "You were supposed to watch it," he whispered as loud as he dared.

We both gave him *the vicki* and pushed our way into the Gents. We took a cubicle each and sat down.

"Can you believe that guy," said Andy through the thin partition, "actually got a shag on the ferry?"

"She must have been at least sixty," I pointed out.

"You think?" he replied. "I tell you one thing," said Andy, between grunts, "she was married."

"How do you know that?"

"I saw her ring," he said, chuckling to himself.

"Bollocks," I said.

"No," he sniggered, "I can't say I saw her bollocks."

We both began laughing, but stopped suddenly when we heard the door of the 'Gents' creak open again.

I waited until whoever it was finished their three-gallon piss, washed their hands, and struggled out of the door again before I heard Andy say, "That was probably her back in for a slash."

That was it, we both erupted into a fit of giggles.

I could hear Andy pull on the toilet paper. "It's really hard to wipe your arse when you're … laughing."

It was, but I managed somehow; practically falling out of my cubicle before staggering over to the sink.

"Would all passengers please return to the car deck," said a muffled voice.

I splashed my face with water and tried to think what I'd say to Willie. If I wound him up too much, he would probably smack me one, but I had to say something. It was just too good an opportunity to miss.

But Andy beat me to it. "So, Willie," he began, "who was that bloke that came out the toilets in front of you?"

"He was a she," he snapped. "A lonely lass on the high seas. Nothing more."

"She was married," I added.

"So are you," he said, accusingly.

"That's different. I'm separated," I pointed out.

"So was she," he replied, "for about twenty minutes. Her hubby was fast asleep a deck above in the TV Lounge."

I stared at him in disbelief. "You're kidding?"

"He won't be," said Andy. "Just our Donald Duck—now we're going to have a vengeful husband *and* pack of Italians after us." Andy wasn't smirking any more when he said, "Are you sure you don't want to shag the captain while you're at it?" He tapped his watch for effect. "Cause there's probably still time."

"Maybe on the way back," sighed Willie, already tending to his precious bass guitar.

"We're gonna have enough to cope with on this trip without you making enemies every five minutes," said Andy.

"You're over-reacting. The Italians are in the brig and that nice lady is a fuckin' Church of England vicar."

We both stared at him incredulously.

"She's a what?" I said.

"An altar licker," chirped Willie, "so she'll say nothing to no-one. Safe as houses."

"Get it right," said Andy, "you mean she's a 'pie and liquor'."

"Saw that, and did that too," Willie added with a wry smile.

"You dirty bastard," I murmured, part of me in awe of the big, scrawny git. He always had a kind of hypnotic power over women. Not exactly what you'd call handsome, Willie had no shame or embarrassment. He said what he was thinking and either got a slap on the face or a result. I wondered what he had said to a vicar?

Out of nowhere, this horrible, creeping panic hit me. What was Maria up to? Where was she now? We were still technically married. Then a stupid thought jumped into my head: had Maria ever strayed during our marriage? I stared at the dishevelled and debauched-looking Willie. If a lady vicar can have a quickie in a toilet …?

We filed down the steep metal steps that led to the car deck and tried to remember where we'd parked the bloody van.

"It's on the other side," said Andy. "You'd better drive," he said to Willie.

Willie shrugged. "Whatever."

As we squeezed into the Transit, I thought I spied the voluptuous vicar, edging between the cars in front of us. "That's her, isn't it?"

Willie put the key in the ignition and nodded.

"She's coming our way," said Andy.

I saw her dopey-looking husband, a bald man with a big paunch and a scraggly grey beard, trying to keep up as she knocked wing mirrors askew with her ample arse.

"Do you think she looks guilty?" I asked, in a deadpan whisper.

"Thou shalt not commit adultery!" Andy half-shouted.

Her husband gave the van a funny look as they passed by, but the randy rector never even flinched.

"She's done this before," said Andy. "I reckon you were just another notch on her candle stick, my boy," he said to Willie.

"I'm not your fuckin' boy," said Willie, his voice all low and threatening.

"How could she do a thing like that and then preach to all those poor bastards every Sunday?" I interrupted. "She shagged a skinny stranger from Drumchapel in a mingin' toilet while her husband slept the sleep of the innocent just a deck above her in the TV Lounge."

"Did she keep her dog-collar on?" asked Andy.

The ferry doors began to swing open and a slash of blinding light made us wince.

Willie swore and shielded his eyes.

I'd barely slept for a couple of hours, so God knows how many minutes our grumpy driver had notched up. Then again, God probably did know; that and much more besides.

CHAPTER TEN

"So, where's the gig tonight?" I asked Andy.

Willie shook his head, trying to keep his eyes open. It looked like he'd managed a heroic two hours, driving on the wrong side of the road, on the wrong side of tired.

Andy yawned and said, "Lyon. A wedding. We... We can't be late."

"Fuck it," swore Willie, pulling into the side of the road. "That's fuckin' six hours away. I need a fix."

My stomach clenched in panic. "Has he got drugs?" I whispered. "Because if he's got some speed in his guitar case, he's a bigger dick-head than I thought. We could have been searched by Customs or–"

"The drugs weren't in his guitar case," Andy interrupted, a mulish frown forming on his face.

"So you knew about this?" I snapped. "I could have ended up in some French jail. What good would I be to Maria then?"

"Well you didn't, so shut up," said Andy, "the 'whizz' is in the fuel tank. Sniffer dogs can't smell it in there."

Willie appeared at my window with a tiny, cellophane bag containing a few grams of an off-white powder. He waved it like he'd just won a fairground goldfish.

Andy rolled the window down and snatched the bag from him, careful not to snag himself on the tiny fish hook.

"So, you fed it into the fuel pipe with some fishing line, and secured it with that hook at the fuel cap?" I asked.

"Yes, but it has to be a lockable fuel cap," murmured Andy. He rummaged about in the glove compartment until he produced a rusty tea-spoon.

"I thought you stopped that shit after you couldn't get it up?" I said to him.

"Doesn't matter much if I can't get it up these days, mate. My missus is long gone." Andy scooped some up with the teaspoon and then shook half back into the bag. He swallowed it like it was nectar.

"It's good shit," said Willie, his pupils already like saucers. He offered me the spoon. "Come and join the party."

I felt my energy ebbing away. I thought of another six hours on the road and then another three hours singing all the crud of the day. "Fine," I relented.

"And we have an additional pick me up," said Willie, opening the palm of his hand. He held six yellow, oval-shaped tablets. "These bad boys will keep you in wood for a whole weekend, guaranteed."

I declined, but Willie and Andy both downed three each.

"Are you even supposed to take three at once?" I asked, pretty sure they weren't.

Willie shrugged.

Back on the road to Lyon, with the fiery fingers of amphetamine sulphate searing through us, Andy decided to break into the pile of postcards left by Maria.

"Wait a minute, Andy," I nodded at Willie, "I still want to keep this stuff private."

"I told you already. Willie knows the whole thing."

"I know, but..."

Willie frowned. "The cards are the least of your worries."

I stared first at Willie, then at Andy in complete horror. "What?"

"You've no idea what you're getting into, Pal," said Willie, flicking on the indicator.

"What do you mean? I'm just trying to figure things out, that's all."

"Look," said Andy, "Willie's got connections. Where do you think he gets the 'speed' from?"

"I've never wanted to know anything about that," I replied.

"My connections," Willie pressed on, "know all about Maria's family. There's quite a few Italians in Glasgow who still belong to the Mafioso."

"I'm not daft, Willie," I said.

"That is a matter of opinion," said Willie. He hit the accelerator and drifted over to the wrong side of the road, narrowly missing a motorcyclist.

"Watch where you're going!" yelled Andy.

"I'll tell you where we're going," said Willie, beads of sweat forming on his neck, "we're going into the belly of the fuckin beast."

"What are you on about?" I moaned, the rush of blood to my brain sharpening my fear.

Andy punched the air. "Tell him, Willie." Before Willie could, Andy turned to me and said, in a machine gun delivery, "Willie is a 'Marvin'. Not like Hank, more like Fred. Fred Marvin. You know. The gangster from Cardonald."

"I know he's a Marvin ..." And then it dawned on me. I'd always known Willie's second name but I hadn't linked him directly to the Marvins in Glasgow, the ones that were always on the news ... "The one who had a book written about him? The 'Stonemaker'? As in the head-stone maker? Fred Marvin is Willie's uncle?"

"He lives in Spain now," said Willie, dismissively.

"But the Marvins are some family," added Andy.

"Maria Saviano is part of a family too," explained Willie. "They own land in Sardinia and Sicily. Your wife is mixed up in some heavy shit." Willie hit the accelerator again.

I sighed. "Can you drop the American gangster crap, Willie? Talk Scottish."

"There's more to your so-called marriage than you think," he continued, now tapping out a complicated rhythm with his fingers on the steering wheel.

"Like what?" I pressed.

"That's what my uncle is trying to find out," said Willie.

"Jesus, I'd rather your uncle kept out of this."

"Better to know as much as possible," said Andy. "Speaking of which..." He peeled another postcard from the top of the pile. "This one is from..." he turned it over to look at the picture, "Majorca?"

Just then, a white sports car estate pulled alongside the van and levelled up. We all stared.

"What's he doing?" barked Willie, swerving towards him.

"Jesus! Willie! Don't fucking do anything stupid!"

The white sports car veered away, then drew up to the window again. I saw the back glass roll down. A man had his arm outstretched.

"They've got a gun!" I yelled.

This time, Willie braked and the white sports car shot forward–but only for a few seconds.

Paranoia kicked in. The speed had me delirious. This couldn't be happening.

"Calm down," said Andy, "there's no gun."

The white sports car was soon level with the passenger window again.

A bullet shattered the rear-view mirror.

"Fuck!" yelled Willie.

There was a massive bang, a sickening crunch of metal, and the roar of a powerful engine. Smoke filled the Transit as we skidded towards the grassy verge. Willie was covering his eyes. I felt the back end of the van shudder, so I grabbed the wheel, jabbed my foot down on the clutch and yanked on the handbrake. We spun a full 360 degrees before rumbling to a halt.

I could taste blood in my mouth and I was convinced I'd been hit.

"What the fuck did you do?" yelled Willie.

I waved the smoke away from my face. "I stopped us from being scrunched, you ungrateful bastard."

"Did you see that?" gasped Andy.

"That white sports car is toast," panted Willie.

Ahead of us, the mangled wreckage of a white sports car estate was scattered over a good hundred yards of the A7. I stared at the body in the middle of the road, barely able to process the mess of flesh and limbs. Cars and lorries swerved round the obstacle as they braked and skidded.

We stumbled out onto the hard shoulder.

My phone rang.

Andy and Willie were standing beside me on the siding, shivering in the cold air.

Willie reached inside the Transit and plucked my phone from the smoke-filled cabin.

Shaking and feeling sick, I pressed it to my ear. "Hello?"

The voice, female and foreign, was somehow familiar. "Get back in your van and drive!"

"What?"

The line went dead.

"Who was it?" asked Andy.

I shrugged. "They told us to get back into the van and drive."

So, as the traffic all around us slowed, we climbed inside our foul-smelling Transit, which started first time, and weaved our way past the wreckage. Amazingly, a man was hanging onto a barrier a few feet from the wreckage. Covered in blood, but still alive.

It had all happened so quickly, but we all agreed that a juggernaut of some description had pulverised the white sports car just as they had begun firing. Slammed into the back of it and continued on through the debris regardless.

About ten miles further on, I looked at the guys' stunned faces. "Where did the lorry come from?" I asked.

"Fuck knows," said Willie. "There's a service station up ahead."

Willie was shaking like a bastard and I felt sick. Andy looked terrible.

"Are you alright?"

"Yeah," said Andy. "But I think I've shit myself. Let's stop."

A motorcycle raced passed us as we climbed the embankment towards the service station. I watched it pull into the garage forecourt–but it didn't fill up. Instead, the rider parked it at the side of the building and went around the back.

I was totally on edge. Whizz always affected me badly. I should never have taken it. It made me paranoid. It felt like a movie.

The van edged into a parking bay. I got out, still convinced I was about to be shot, but I couldn't stop myself.

"Ian!" shouted Willie. "Snap out of it."

"I'm going to the bogs," said Andy.

I turned back to face the guys. "Maybe I need something in my stomach." Jumpy as hell, I carried on towards the shop at the edge of the forecourt. I prised a few euros from my jeans and looked about for something I could afford.

"Donuts?" said a voice.

I saw a girl, who looked to be in her mid-twenties, nod at an orange, hand-written sign that read, 'offre special'.

The donuts were about all I could afford. "Yes, why not?"

Andy stepped in behind me. "You pulled already?" He winked

at me. Willie appeared at his side.

I floundered.

The girl laughed and said, "He has not 'pulled', as you say."

Her accent was unmistakably French. She had long, dark hair and a lithe grace about her. She moved like a delicate bird as she walked over to the donuts and picked them up. Andy and myself stood frozen to the spot, gawping like a couple of idiots as she tossed the pack across to us.

"Where are you headed?" she asked.

"Tell her fuck all." Willie snatched the donuts from my hand, eyeing the girl suspiciously.

She tilted her head at Willie and bit down on a smile before saying, "You must be the awkward one. Let me see," she continued, "you are good in bed, but lousy at just about everything else."

I found myself nodding unconsciously.

She beckoned us away from a few truckers who were becoming interested in our conversation. She pointed a me and said, in a quiet, alluring voice, "I am to be your bodyguard."

My mouth fell open. "Sorry? I didn't quite catch that."

"Are you on the game?" Willie asked, suddenly brightening.

"No, I am not," she snapped.

"Just say that last bit again," I said. "The bit before he..." I nodded at Willie.

"I am to be your bodyguard," she repeated.

I laughed, but she wasn't laughing back. Her face expression hardened.

"Why would he need a body guard?" asked Andy.

"Because three men in a white sports car pulled alongside your van one mile before you pulled into the rest area and tried to shoot you."

There was a long pause before I said, "And you know this, because…?"

"I know this," she said, smugly, "because I was the one who saved your life."

CHAPTER ELEVEN

Lorene Duval sounded more like the name of a movie star than a bodyguard. She seemed precocious, beautiful and–apparently–deadly. No more than five foot three, she reminded me of a heron poised to strike.

"So who do you work for?" I asked, bursting with questions.

"I don't know," said Lorene, "and I prefer it that way."

I exhaled in frustration, my follow up questions instantly useless.

"So how did you get here?" asked Andy. "We saw the lorry race ahead."

Willie nodded. "The motorbike. She's wearing leathers."

"Very good, Mr Marvin."

Willie's eyes narrowed.

"You know his name?" I broached.

"And much more besides," she answered.

After some debate on the garage forecourt, Willie and Andy gave the nod to let her come along, probably for all the wrong reasons. So now we were all back in the van heading for Leon with Lorene.

We passed the lorry. It was parked on the hard shoulder, its roller door fully open, a metal ramp sticking out the back. A gendarme was talking into his phone, the blue light on his bike blinking.

After an hour or two, Willie shot her a sly glance in the rear-view mirror. "For all we know you could be some kind of stalker. Maybe you saw the incident with the white sports car and the truck, then just decided to follow us."

"I might have," she answered, nonplussed.

"How do we know that it was you driving the truck?" pressed Andy. He twisted round to talk to us.

"You don't," she said.

"What else do you know about us?" I asked.

"Some things," she replied.

"Since the words blood and stone come to mind," said Andy, "how about I help you along a bit?"

She shrugged, lifting her heavy holdall up onto her knees. "Whatever."

Andy grinned as he rummaged in his bag. He pulled out the bundle of postcards that Maria had sent to Julie.

"No," I protested.

"Yes!" said Andy and Willie.

I would have told them to fuck off, but weirdly, we'd all stopped swearing since Lorene had appeared.

"So," began Andy, "just to bring you up to date, Ian has been dumped by his wife Maria after ten years of marriage. In one night, she emptied his house and disappeared back to her homeland–Sardinia."

"We think. I'm not sure we should reveal too much," I said.

"I know all of this," said Lorene. "Maria Saviano is to marry Franco Galdini. Two Mafia families will unite and stop years of bloodshed."

"Eh… Can I just stop you there." My heart was pounding, and not just from the effects of the speed, which still tore at my senses and made everything so much more intense. "Maria is married to me."

"Maybe," said Lorene. "Do you have the certificate?"

"No," I floundered, "Maria has all that stuff."

"Maybe," she said, one more time.

"So who was the guy that warned us off?" said Andy. His words spilled out in a jerking staccato fashion that made Lorene narrow her eyes.

"He had the name Azuni on his van," I added.

She shrugged and said, "I don't know, but the Azunis work for the Savianos. They always work for the Savianos."

Willie's eyes were wide as he drove. He didn't say much, but I could see the gears grinding behind them.

"So," interrupted Andy, "that Azuni guy gave us these." He waved the postcards. "He told us not to follow Maria–"

"- or we would be killed," I added.

"But he gave us these." Andy waved the cards again. "Postcards that Maria sent to a friend. Holidays and stuff over the years that–"

"- that give some insight into how she was thinking and into Ian's personality?" finished Lorene.

We all stared at her for a moment. It was probably only a second, but due to the speed racing through us it felt like an hour.

"Let me hear one," said Lorene.

Andy and myself twisted around in our seats and Andy held up a postcard that said, 'Majorca'.

I shrugged. "It was like a honeymoon. We couldn't afford to go anywhere posh."

"She had plenty of money," mumbled Willie, seemly knowing better.

"We were skint," I crossed my arms. "No matter what your crazy uncle tells you."

Andy tapped the card, "Now, now, ladies–listen and learn."

On the postcard, I recognized the pine trees that surrounded the 'Los Mollinos Hotel'. I could almost smell their scent, taste the cool sangria that the waiters served beside the pool. I could also feel the 'wiz' racing up the arteries on the side of my head. My scalp tingled. "That was ages ago."

"Eight years ago," said Andy. He read out the card:

"Dear Julie, thanks for looking after our dog, Charlie. I should never have let Ian persuade me to leave him behind. I burst into tears as soon as I sat down on the plane."

I closed my eyes as I remembered the resentment that had oozed from the air stewardess on that flight. She'd asked Maria if she was ok.

"No," Maria had sobbed, "he made me leave my baby... with a friend for two weeks so he could take me somewhere hot and..."

'Shag my brains out', she may as well have finished. The air hostess thudded my beer down so hard on my flip table that it fizzed up and streamed, like a soda fountain, all over my jeans.

Andy continued:

"We went out to see the Drifters last night and Ian got legless. On the way home, he chatted up the holiday rep and told the whole bus that they were shit singers, unlike him, as he was a pop star. He then crawled up the front steps of the hotel, giggling like Norman Wisdom and passed out before he reached our room. So much for 'sex on the beach'.

Bastard.

Wish I was back home... Again.

Maria.

Andy and Willie 'tut tutted' like a couple of matrons.

"Give me that!" I said, snatching the card from Andy. I read it again, half expecting it to be at least a partial wind up, but it wasn't. It was in Maria's handwriting and it had been read out verbatim.

Lorene gave a little tight-lipped shake of head, clearly unimpressed. "You were very immature."

"She enjoyed that holiday," I protested. "Apart from leaving our dog, Charlie, behind'," I added sulkily.

"Seems to me," said Willie, "that you didn't know fuck all about Maria. How she felt, where she came from, or who she was."

"We had ten years of married bliss!" I snapped. The speed had me in its grip, but through the sparks of exhilaration that fried the neurons in my brain, I glimpsed little fragments of my life with Maria and wondered if the whole thing had really been a sham.

It couldn't have been.

Not all of it.

* * *

By the time we got to Lyon it was raining hard. The sky was bearing down on the city like a lead shroud and the effects of the 'speed' we'd gulped down after the ferry was beginning to ease.

"We either ride out the storm, or we top up," said Willie, his eyes sagging like a couple of overfilled shopping bags.

"I say we top up," said Andy. He shuffled in his seat awkwardly and pulled his jumper down over his jeans.

I noticed a sizeable lump in Andy's trousers as his jumper rode up again. "For God's sake," I moaned, shifting further along my seat, "we have a lady present."

Andy shrugged. "Bloody thing won't go away."

"Same here," said Willie. He let out a burst of laughter. "Told you about the wood. Those tabs counteract the 'whizz'. I say we top up with the last of the 'sulph' and go on the hunt for some French totty, fully armed." He glanced at Lorene. "No disrespect intended." He hesitated for a moment and then added, "Not unless you fancy … you know?"

Lorene leaned over and caught Willie's hair from the back. She twisted it and whispered something in his ear.

"Argh!" he yelled, shaking his head and righting the steering wheel. "I'll take that as a maybe then." A glimmer of a smile returned to his face.

"Take is as a 'never'," replied Lorene.

I shuffled a little further away from Lorene. "We should never have taken that stuff. I feel as if my heart is gonna explode at any moment."

"Why did you take speed?" asked Lorene.

"Because we wanted to," said a Willie.

Lorene shrugged. "You know it can kill you, right?"

"This is killing me. It isn't going down," wheezed Andy.

Lorene eased back in her seat. "You must have taken something else."

"They did," I explained.

Willie shook his head. "I don't care if your bodyguard is here, I've had this bad boy since Reims and it's fuckin' painful."

"What happens if it stays there for two days?" Andy asked, wide-eyed.

"You'll both die," Lorene explained.

"Great," moaned Willie, "Cause of death–rampant 'stonner'. The poor undertaker won't be able to shut the coffin. They'll need to bury us face down."

Andy began rummaging in his holdall. "Maybe if we take another teaspoon of speed it'll put it away?"

"Maybe if you take another spoonful of speed you'll die on the spot," I added. "Whizz and Wood obviously don't mix."

"That's it," announced Willie, "I'm gonna pull over and have a wank."

Lorene rolled her eyes.

I felt my neck go hot with embarrassment. "Willie, for God's sake..."

"Pull over," snapped Andy. He was clutching his heart.

Willie slammed on the brakes and screeched to a halt.

"Jesus!" I shouted. "You can't just..."

"That's why it's called the hard shoulder," said Willie, not a glimmer of humour in his tone.

"Guys?" I couldn't believe it. We were on one of the busiest motorways in France.

They both jumped out and went round the side of the van, cars and lorries thundering past.

I glanced at Lorene.

"Why do you hang out with those crazy bastards?" she sighed.

I leaned out of the window. Both of them were chugging away for dear life, trousers at their knees. "I suppose you want me to put the fucking hazard triangle up?" I shouted.

Andy gave me a thumbs up with his free hand.

The van shook each time a lorry passed and I kept a nervous eye on the passenger-side wing mirror for any gendarme. As I waited in my own little hell, the inevitable aftermath that always followed 'speed' kicked in'; the total and utter, zombie-like exhaustion crept over me like a heavy fog. Shivering, I leaned out of the window again in time to see Willie pull his kecks up and amble back. Andy was still going at it. He looked over his shoulder at me like a man possessed. "Got any mucky pictures of Maria?"

"Piss off, you dirty little—"

The driver door squeaked open and Willie jumped in. He thumped the steering wheel. "It's still there."

I bit down my lip to stop myself from laughing.

Andy's door opened seconds later. "It's no good," he wailed. "I can't concentrate."

"Eh... If you boys are quite finished, we should get a move on. And look," I pointed at the traffic ahead, "now there's been a crash or something. The road is jamming up big time."

Willie indicated and pulled out onto the busy dual carriageway. "Give me more wiz, Andy. I'm gonna risk it."

"We'll make it to Marseille on time if we drive straight there after the wedding," reasoned Andy. "We can kip in the queue for the ferry."

"It's your funeral," I muttered.

"It will be easier for me to do my job if they are both dead anyway," said Lorene, quite matter-of-factly.

"Charming," said Andy.

"Right, Andy," said Willie, "where's this French wedding?"

Andy squinted down at his mobile and read out the text from the booking agent: "it's just off the Place Aristide Briand. A restaurant called Fifi's. There!" Andy pointed to a signpost for the D74, but the queue looked even worse that way, so we went down towards the D966 instead.

Our window wipers were on overdrive when we pulled up outside Fifi's. Through the bleary windscreen the venue looked a bit on the small side. I could see that it was packed, and there was a damp, tell-tale trail of confetti leading up to the front door. I could also see something else. There was another van parked up at the fire exit.

I saw Willie's eyes narrow. "We better not be double booked," he growled.

A couple of young guys bounced out of the fire exit and returned to the other van's opened back doors. They hauled out a bass speaker and a bagful of stands.

"I'll go and have a word," said Willie.

"Just go easy," warned Andy.

"Why don't you go, Andy," I whispered. "You know what Willie can be like." We didn't need another fight on our hands.

Andy answered in an anxious voice, "I can't go outside out yet."

"What?" I hesitated for a second before glancing down at Andy's straining jeans. "Jesus! Give me a break."

"I'm good now," said Willie. "That second spoon of speed did the trick."

I could see how tense and totally wired Willie was. "Willie," I warned, "keep it calm."

Lorene pushed Willie's seat forward and followed him outside. She turned back to me. "Don't move."

I put my hands up. "Fine."

Willie returned all flustered. "We're double booked alright, and they're pulling the old 'we were here first' rule." He opened the passenger door and stared at Andy. "It's your booking. You better go and speak to someone before I crack a few heads."

We both stared at Andy until he relented and jumped out of the van.

"Go on, 'Robocock'! Knock em dead!" jeered Willie. He turned back to look at me. "Ha ha. Where's your bird?"

There was no sign of Lorene.

Andy waddled off into battle.

A lady, about sixty or so, with a white rose in the lapel of her dress, appeared at the fire exit. We could see her arguing with Andy, trying her best not to look down, glancing this way and that. Within seconds her face was like a baboon's arse: puffy and rouge, so we knew she was going to buckle. "Anything! Just set up at the other end of the restaurant!" we heard her yelp.

Andy turned to face us and gave us the thumbs up.

We tried our best to set up our equipment while Andy tried his best to hide his hard-on, walking in and out with a drum case strategically positioned or a coat held at a stupid angle. There was still no sign of Lorene.

The other band were more of a disco outfit and, since it seemed there was no issue in paying us both our fee, we came to an arrangement about who would play when.

The guests were mostly English, with just a smattering of locals.

"The other band are Italian," I pointed out.

"Yeah..." mused Andy, distractedly. He was literally tapping his hard-on with a drum stick.

"Are you gonna mic that thing up?" said Willie.

"Ha-fuckin-ha," replied Andy. He stared at us, a bewildered look on his face. "It's just not going to go down, is it?"

"Not until somebody else does first," sneered Willie.

"Even then," whined Andy. "What if it stays this way for ever?"

We ended up having more than a few drinks with the Italian band, who were called 'Gellata'. They were all pretty cool apart from the singer who was a complete weirdo. He never really said much or even looked at us.

After they played the first set their keyboard player introduced us as 'Robocock', and we kicked off with 'Sweet Home Alabama'.

During the buffet, I watched Andy and Willie move in on a

few good-looking stragglers. I was just about to go over and join them when I felt a tap on my shoulder. Half-hoping it was Lorene, I turned around and came face to face with the weird singer from the other band. "We need to talk," he said.

"Don't worry, we're both going to get paid," I said, worried that he was going to hassle me about the money.

"It's not that," he said.

"You should go back to Scotland," he said.

I looked at him for a long moment before saying, "What makes you say that?"

"You don't know who you're dealing with," he continued. "They will kill you if you continue to look for your wife. The Galdinis, the Savianos … even the Azunis, they are all out for you."

"What? How do you …?" but he'd walked off, leaving his unfinished drink at the bar.

I didn't understand how some random singer could know anything about my situation, about Maria. I thought of interrupting Andy and Willie, going over to their table and pulling them to their feet, but what would be the point? Why spoil their night? We still had another hour to play. We still had to step up the pace, turn it up a few notches and then finish with, as instructed, the customary–'Auld Lang Syne'.

I looked across the dance floor towards the opposite end of the large restaurant and saw that 'Gellata' were already packing up, quietly lifting their gear through the bustling crowd. We had ten minutes before we were due to play so I went over to speak to them.

The lead singer had disappeared, but their bass player and keyboard player were still busy dismantling their equipment.

"Could I speak to you for a minute?" I asked.

They both paused, nervously looking about them for any sign of their lead singer.

"I think he's gone," I said, "but I wondered if you could tell me more?"

"We don't know nothing," said the wiry-looking bass player.

"Tino got a call when you were playing your set," said the keyboard player. He was thick set and had the beginnings of a paunch.

The bass player gave him a jarring glance.

"People know that you are going to Sardinia," he said.

"What people?" I asked.

The bass player strolled off, clearly done with the conversation.

"Tino said that Carlos Azuni had called him."

I felt my head pound even harder. Was this the same Azuni, the man who threatened me on my doorstep, the one who had warned us that we'd be killed if we followed him? How could he know where we were?

"Who booked you for this wedding?" I asked, not entirely sure what I wanted to glean from the question.

"Azuni," said the bass player. "We only got the booking at four o'clock today. Azuni is Tino's cousin. He told Tino to tell the Mother of the Bride that you weren't going to turn up and that we would do the gig for nothing, as a favour."

I followed him outside as he carried a four by twelve speaker cabinet out to his van.

"Why wouldn't we have turned up?" I asked.

"This morning ... you should have been ..."

"Killed by the men in a white sports car?" I finished.

He hesitated. "You should go home."

"Who was in the white sports car? And how do you even know about it?"

I pulled back as the keyboard player stepped out of the shadows. He caught me by the shoulder. "Azuni is old-school Mafioso," he whispered. "He is a lieutenant for the Savianos. The most powerful Family in Europe. It's his job to know everything. "Your wife is lost. She is not coming back."

"What have you done to her?" I brushed his hand off my shoulder.

The keyboard player, his expression fixed in tight-lipped determination said, almost fearfully, "Nothing. Absolutely nothing." He showed me his palms of his hands, as if in surrender and backed off. "She was always going to go back home."

Soon, I found myself alone in the dark alley beside a pink neon sign that flashed–Fifi's. The acrid smell of exhaust fumes wafted over me as the sound of laughter drifted out of the restaurant into the night.

"Ian?"

It was Lorene. She was strobed in a rose-coloured wash that gave her a cartoon-like appearance. I wondered what she'd heard, what else she knew.

"So, you knew about these guys?" I asked.

"You need to decide how much you want your wife back," she said. Her tone was seductive, the words sounding more like a proposition than a statement.

"I ... I'm confused."

"About what?" she pressed.

"About this whole bloody thing." wondering if there was even the slightest chance a woman like Lorene could ever fall for me. Why was I even thinking about this woman in that way when I was doing all this for Maria. "So, the whole Mafia bit is true?"

"Of course it is. Maria Saviano was always going to marry Franco Galdini. There's too much at stake. I can't see how you can stop her."

"Who is protecting me?"

"Me."

"No, I mean ..."

"We're on!" Andy caught hold of my shoulder, nodded at Lorene, and led me back inside.

CHAPTER TWELVE

I thought long and hard about what to do next. It was three in the morning. Andy and Willie, off with a couple of bridesmaids, were still pushing their heart function to the limits. Here in the van it was just me, wide-eyed and exhausted, staring at Lorene who was sleeping on the back seat. I looked at her smooth complexion in the dim light and wondered what horrors this gorgeous creature had seen in her past.

Why had she chosen to be an assassin or bodyguard, or whatever the hell she was? Obviously lethal and intelligent, right now she looked like an angel, like butter wouldn't melt in her mouth. God, she was beautiful.

There I was, off on some wild goose chase after a woman who had ditched me for another life and, most probably, another man –looking lustfully at a girl quite a bit younger than me and well out of my reach. Kidding myself, that's what I was doing. I was good at that. I was an ok guitarist, an alright singer, but bloody brilliant at kidding myself.

I found the key that Maria had returned to me and turned it over in my cramping fingers. It was cold to the touch, almost sticky. I wondered if the old man on Dead Dog Beach had actually known Maria back then. Ten years ago... Had he given her the key for a reason, or was it just a random event?

At that moment, a wave of speed-induced paranoia crashed through my mind, filling my head with visions of hidden assassins and heartless hit men. I pulled my knees up to my chest and groped about for the edge of my blanket, shivering in the damp confines of the van.

"Hey!" said a voice at my window.

I almost pissed my pants.

"It's us," said Willie, a glaikit grin fixed upon his face.

Great, I thought, our driver is drugged up, drunk and delirious. I tried to keep the venom out of my voice as I explained how I'd single-handedly stripped down the band gear and loaded it into the van. "And now, by the looks of you two, I'm going to have to drive to Marseille."

I slid into the driver's seat and started the engine.

Andy peered over at Lorene. "Did you give her one, then?" he whispered.

"No, I did not," I spat back. "I'm not a fuckin' animal like you."

"But you want to, don't you?" Willie interjected, a bit too loud for my liking.

I glanced over the seat at Lorene, still seemingly sleeping in the shadows.

"She's very beautiful," I replied, in a half-trance, exhaustion making me careless. "Stunning and intelligent."

"Ah," said Andy, "that's what you used to say about Maria."

"I did?" I replied, not remembering any such thing.

Squinting out at the main street, a brightly lit road sign said, 'Marseille 313km', which, all being well, translated into three hours in the Transit.

It was then, my head still pounding with paranoia, that I decided our van was rigged. A bomb was probably linked to the ignition and we would all be blown to pieces. *Should I wake Lorene?*

"What's wrong?" said Andy.

"Nothing." Full of insane bravado and not wanting to embarrass myself by suggesting such a stupid notion to Lorene, I turned the ignition and closed my eyes. I waited for the customary stall of the engine, like in the movies, before a car bomb explosion… but nothing happened. The old Transit, solid and reliable, purred out of the alley and into the night.

Willie and Andy were already bragging about their hook-ups.

I thought about interrupting the boys' gynaecology lesson, dropping the bombshell that I was thinking about turning round and going home. But I didn't. I saw the exit for the A7 Sud and brought us up to sixty miles per hour.

I always thought there was something magical about driving home after a gig. We weren't exactly 'driving home' this time, but the feeling was still there. We had money in our pockets, we'd watched people enjoy themselves. And now, in the afterglow, I could tell we all felt the same. In that moment, still damp with sweat, we knew that this is what we were born to do.

A few hours later I felt as if I was going to fall asleep. I turned to Andy. I felt I should tell him what had happened. "I was warned not to drive on to Marseille," I explained. "The other band knew all about Maria. They said that we weren't supposed to make it to that wedding."

"The white sports car?" said Andy.

"We're going to need reinforcements," said Willie.

"Lots," added Andy.

There was no movement on the back seat. "We've got Lorene," I whispered, mostly to myself. I felt as though there was a jack-hammer mounted on my head. My legs were shaking so much I could barely keep my feet on the pedals.

Willie shook his head. "Where was she, anyway? She disappeared during the gig."

"Watching us from afar," I lied. I had no idea where she'd got to, but I felt I should somehow protect her. "She saved our lives."

Willie raised his eyebrows and glared at me. "So *she* says."

"Look, we can turn back right now," I relented, "Go back to Scotland. No hard feelings."

"Fuck off," sneered Willie. "Mafia or no Mafia, we're going to sort this out. Those bastards tried to kill me."

Andy didn't look so convinced.

"The way I see it," I continued, accelerating onwards, "is that we seem to have some friends as well as some enemies. That band tried to warn us to stay away."

"Who else is out to help us then, apart from sleeping beauty and that band?" said Andy.

There was a pause before I said, "Well, somebody must have hired Lorene to protect us."

"Look after you," reminded Willie.

"I suppose that guy Azuni gave us the postcards," said Andy.

"And Maria gave me the key," I added.

"That was a 'fuck off key', not a 'here's some help key," said Willie.

"What are you talking about, Willie?"

Willie shrugged.

"Show Willie the key," said Andy.

"Why?"

"Because we're driving into a war and I want to know as much as possible."

I took it, with one hand, from a recess on the dash, and handed it to Willie.

He drew his head back, squinting. "Fuck me."

"What is it?" I said.

Willie didn't answer. Instead, he wrestled with his jacket until he found his own keys–shamble of brass and steel. He prized them apart, shook them manically, and peeled one away from the bunch. His face twisted into a smirk. "Snap!"

CHAPTER THIRTEEN

The key that sparkled in Willie's spider-like fingers was, as far as I could see, identical to the one Maria had returned during our fateful meal.

"Do you know what this is for?" asked Willie.

"Of course I don't know," I replied. My eyes darted between Willie and the road.

Despite our predicament, he had that same smug, aloof face on. "I got my key in Rome. At my uncle's stag night."

"The gangster one?" I asked.

"Uncle Fred? Aye. This key is for a locker in one of the most upmarket casinos in Rome. But get this – if you show them the key, you can get a free room."

"Why would your dodgy uncle give you the key?" pressed Andy.

"My uncle gave it to me, because I was the only one at his stag who was flesh and blood."

"So you can get free digs in the casino anytime you want?"

"How do you know it's the same kind of key?" I cut in, seeing Willie's expression.

"There is a letter 'R' on the bow of the key," explained Willie.

Andy, his eyes still wide and black with whizz, grunted in frustration. "You worked in that wee shop on the High Street. The one that cut keys and fixed shoes, didn't you?"

I knew the one he meant, and I had a vague recollection of Willie working there when we formed our first band.

"Uncle Fred got me the job," explained Willie.

"I bet he did," I said. "*Handy.*"

"Anyway the 'R' stands for 'Redante'. It was named after the first ever casino."

I could almost see the cogs turning in Willie's head.

"The first Redante was built about four hundred years ago," he explained, "but the new one is the dog's bollocks."

"A known gangster took you on his stag do, and you were

happy to go?" asked Andy.

"He's a nice guy," protested Willie.

"Sure," said Andy.

"Whoa there, cowboy." I sat forward, gripping the wheel. "Hang on a minute. Are you telling me that ten years ago, a dead dog washed up–on our beach–with this exact kind of key around its neck?"

Andy whistled. "That's fucked up."

Willie just shrugged. "It wasn't your own fuckin' personal beach."

"I know that," I replied, "but–"

"Wait a minute," interrupted Andy. "What if the dog belonged to some 'big shot'? Someone who, like Willie's uncle Fred, had the money to be a member of that casino in Rome?"

"But why would he keep a key like that round a dog's neck?" I said.

"A souvenir? I don't know. Willie had his key in the pocket of his mingin' jeans," said Andy.

"They're not mingin'," said Willie indignantly.

"When was the last time you wore anything else?" pressed Andy.

The question lay unanswered for a good three hours.

I counted down the kilometres until I saw the sign for the Vieux-Port du Marseille. "You two still awake?" I asked, squinting at Willie and the key he clutched in his sweaty hand. "That posh casino of yours isn't going to keep a room ready for you forever, right?"

Willie shrugged again. "Uncle Fred said that our keys would only work for the week."

"Exactly," barked Andy.

"But he also said," continued Willie, "that there were some rooms on tap for years. On the last night, he pointed out an old guy at the roulette wheel. He told us that he was one of the super-rich. He wore one of those shiny suits, dark glasses, had a couple of young things standing either side of him, like in the Bond films … the whole shebang."

The boulevard sloped towards the ferry port, the road bathed in the early light. I noticed a row of tall palms lining the pavement, their fronds whispered in the warm breeze, like silent sentries watching our every move. I thought about Maria. Was she under guard in some Sardinian safe-house? Or was she sunbathing with not a care in the world, glad to be free of me? "Do you think Maria is ok?" I broached.

"She went of her own accord," said Andy. "I reckon," he continued, "that we should throw them off our trail. Everyone thinks we're going to Sardinia, so let's go somewhere else."

"But your agent's already got us those gigs in Sardinia," said Willie.

"But the first gig isn't for another three days," Andy reminded him.

I pulled over into parking place. I could see the ferry, 'The Sardinian Warrior', looming high above the terminal about half a mile away. "

"In the light of this 'key business', I think we should go to Rome?" said Andy. "Get one over on them."

"How?" I protested, panic building in my chest.

"Let's go to the Redante and try the key," said Willie.

"Don't be so bloody stupid," I said.

"What's the worst that can happen?" said Andy, "We get to Rome and find that the key doesn't work. Or maybe it still opens a locker with something in it that will give us the upper hand."

"I suppose it might throw them off our trail for a bit."

"We'll get to eat great pizza and go to the Colosseum," added Willie.

"We might even get a gig?" said Andy, opening his mobile.

Willie stopped playing with his key, reached over, and closed Andy's mobile. "Fuck the agent getting a cut. I'll get us a gig."

Maria still lingered in my head, a ghost I couldn't shake. Was she hiding out in some Sardinian safe house, waiting for me to save her? Or was she already moving on–drinking wine under the sun, laughing, forgetting? I tried to concentrate. "I suppose we might be able to find out who bought the 'dead dog key' in the first place. Who the old man was."

"Rome?" prompted Willie.

"Fine," I said reluctantly.

"We can drive there," said Willie.

I yawned. "You can drive there. I need a kip."

"Fine," said Willie, "but I want to stretch out for a bit too."

We both craned our necks looking over at the sleeping Lorene.

"What about her?" said Willie, a mischievous smile forming on his skull-like face.

"Just leave her," I warned.

Willie narrowed his eyes. "Are you falling for your babysitter?"

"Keep it down," I whispered.

"We'll take that's a yes then," added Andy.

"So, what's the point of this whole fuckin' trip?" said Willie. "I mean, if you fancy her."

Lorene stirred.

"I thought you wanted your misses back?"

"I do," I whispered.

With the whizz almost out of my system exhaustion washed over me like a big lazy wave.

Willie was already sleeping.

Andy was still wired.

* * *

"I've been staring at that ferry for four fuckin' hours," said Andy.

I was sweating like mad, dizzy and starving. I stared hard at Andy. "You didn't sleep?"

Like a mummy rising from the tomb, Willie sat bolt upright and climbed over into the driver's seat.

I spun round to face him. "You went over into the back?"

Andy laughed. "You think he snuggled into Lorene, don't you?"

"No... I..."

Willie stretched. "I never touched her. She pissed off about three hours ago."

"Where to?" I asked, scanning the ferry terminal.

The passenger side door opened and I almost fell out onto the road.

"Jesus!"

"No, not him. It's just me," said Lorene. She pointed up at the ferry. "So, we go?"

"Ah... Well... There's been a change of plan," I began.

"Really?" said Lorene. "I thought you wanted to chase your wife down and beg her to come back."

Willie and Andy both smirked, no doubt eager to hear my reply.

I paused, suddenly annoyed. "It's not about begging her back."

"Yes, it is," quipped Andy.

"We've decided that he can beg her back after we've been to Rome," added Willie.

"Maria gave me a key."

Lorene's brow furrowed. "What key?"

Willie tossed it to Andy, who passed it back.

Lorene turned it over in her palm. "The Redante?"

I groaned. "Does everyone know about the bloody key apart from me?"

Lorene squinted at me. "You're going to drive into the belly of the beast?"

"What?"

"At the moment, the Redante is run by the Azuni family on behalf of the Savianos. The Azunis are like..." She seemed to be searching for the right word.

"Slaves," said Willie.

"No... No, more like, henchmen. They tidy things up for Charles Saviano. Look after his assets too. But things are changing..."

I was amazed that Lorene knew so much about the Mafia. But then, why should I be. She'd probably worked for them in the past.

"What's changing?" asked Willie.

Lorene sighed. "After years of war between the Galdinis and the Savianos, it's rumoured that they got together to eliminate four judges that were closing in on all Mafia interests in Southern Europe."

"Sounds weird," said Willie.

Lorene folded her arms. "It's called a 'trophy truce'."

Andy frowned. "A what?"

Willie rolled his eyes. "It's when two gangs team up to take out a bigger threat." He nodded at Lorene. .

Lorene nodded back.

I stared at Willie. "How the heck do you know all this stuff?"

"Willie's right," said Lorene, "but they took the truce a bit further."

"They decided on a marriage of convenience," said Willie.

Lorene pushed her lips together and nodded at Willie. "He's good."

I wasn't sure if she was impressed or just surprised Willie wasn't completely full of shit.

I watched Lorene stretch. "If the Savianos and the Galdinis join forces, they will become the most powerful outfit in the region."

"So... the Redante?" I pressed.

"Is to be run by the Galdinis after they join forces." finished Lorene. "That's what I hear."

"So, my Maria marrying Franco is part of the plan?"

"Always was," added Andy.

"And you, Mr Showbiz, played your own part to a tee," said Willie.

"What part?"

"The stooge,' said Andy.

"A guy so far up his own arse that he would never see any of this coming," said Willie.

I looked to Lorene for some support, but she was already digging into her bag for new clothes. As she rummaged she said, "Sardinia or Rome?"

Andy and Willie waited for my reply.

"Rome."

CHAPTER FOURTEEN

Was Willie right? Was I beginning to fall for Lorene? It might suit Maria if I did. It might suit everyone if I did. I moved into the back seat beside Lorene after we filled up with fuel. I liked being beside her, yeah. But also, weird as fuck, like I was some man-child she'd been hired to babysit.

"You know a lot about the families involved in this whole scenario so you must know something about me too," I said.

"Some things, yes," she replied.

"Let's do another postcard," said Andy. He grunted and reached into his bag, pulling out the bundle of postcards that Maria had sent to her friend, Julie.

"No," I protested. "Not again. Lorene's not interested."

"I am interested," said Lorene. "Read on, Andy."

"Excellent. So, just to recap," continued Andy, "Ian thought he had a great marriage and Maria thought it was shit."

I wanted to smash Andy's face in, right there and then.

"Sad," said Lorene, her eyes still fixed on the road.

Willie had repositioned the shattered rear-view mirror so that he could stare at Lorene's tits.

Andy slipped a postcard free of the pack. "Are you sitting comfortably, Lorene?"

"Mais oui," said Lorene, her voice light and sing-song.

"So, this card is from St Kitts," began Andy.

"Piss off," I mouthed.

"It says–'*Hi Julie...*'" Andy paused and said, "Like I said last time, Julie is the friend that Maria posted all the cards to."

"And Julie is where?" asked Lorene.

"She's dead," I whispered.

"But, of course," answered Lorene.

Andy continued: "*Having a relaxing time here in between the Caribbean and the Atlantic. The all-inclusive holiday camp is basically a holding pen with great eye candy. Yet again, Ian proves to be a bigger 'fanny' than I could ever have imagined. Ha! See how I'm using some Glaswegian*

now? All-inclusive means drinks, food and water sports. Well, Ian got madder and madder each day at the staff on the beach, who all said it was too rough to try anything in the sea, so yesterday he said to this big black guy—
"don't you know who I am?" Then insisted he take him water skiing. Out in the choppy sea, the big black guy hit the full-power button and Ian's arse soon began to act like one of those big, scoopy pelican beaks. His thin trunks had slipped to one side, and he got a free Caribbean enema."

Tears were actually running down Andy's cheeks as he read the last part. I wanted to wipe them off with my fist. *"Ten minutes after his ordeal, while we were talking to a nice American couple, Ian yelped like a seal and ran up the beach. The Caribbean wanted back into the Caribbean again and Ian had to hold back the floodgates while he cycled off into the distance, back to our room."*

"So," said Andy, wiping tears from his eyes, "what's the moral of today's story?"

Lorene raised her neat eyebrows and said, "Try not to be a fanny?" She gave me a series of very attractive little tut tuts.

"It wasn't nice," I remembered out loud.

"It also tells me," continued Lorene, "that your wife had eyes for other men—and perhaps desires."

Something in me twisted and sank. I clenched my jaw and forced a swallow.

"I always thought she might be a bit of a slut," said Willie.

I could see his beady eyes in the remains of the rear-view mirror. "Fuck off, Willie." I glanced at Lorene and was about to apologise for swearing, but she pursed her lips, partly closed her eyes and gave me a little shake of her head. The whole look said, 'There's no need'.

"I always reckoned she fancied me," added Willie, obviously trying to wind me up even more. I could have punched him on the back of the head. Tempting—but probably not a great idea while he had the wheel.

"Lorene might be bang on," said Andy. "Maybe she left you so she could get better at being a slut. Like, become an expert slut, a black belt or something."

Willie chortled, and I smacked Andy over the head.

"Argh! Fuck off," he said, ducking down in his seat.

"When a man sleeps around, he's a bit of a lad. When a woman does it, she's a slut. Funny, that." said Lorene.

"Maria did not sleep around," I pronounced.

"Variety is the spice of life," Willie murmured.

"Shut up, Willie."

"Like, in the morning," Andy continued, still rubbing the back of his head, "did she go straight for the *corn flakes*, or did she pull one of those variety packs out of the cupboard?"

"Piss off, Dr Spock." I slapped him harder this time.

Lorene gave Andy a confused glance.

"No, Andy's right," said Willie, knowing fine-well that he was immune to a good slap because he was driving. "Ian, when Maria bought a pack of chews, did she pick blackcurrant or did she go for the mixed flavours?"

Andy and Willie started laughing harder.

"Will you two stop talking pish?"

Just then, Lorene reached into her holdall and pulled out a handgun.

"Jesus," blurted Andy, raising his hands. "we were only kidding."

I felt my body tense. Lorene moved fast, too fast, sliding over me and priming the gun.

"There's a Merc C class; black, number plate–SR13 088. It's been on our tail for more than twelve kilometres," she said.

"What are you going to do?" I asked.

Lorene put her head between Andy and Willie. "There's another service station in a kilometre. Pull into the picnic area. I'll tell you what to do after that."

I watched her stuff the gun in her belt, then slip in beside Andy in the front seat. She clicked down the door handle as we turned into the picnic area.

"Park up in about a hundred metres," she said. Then, pushing the door open, she leapt out while we were still moving.

Andy reached over and shut the door. "Fuck me," he muttered, "it's Cat Woman."

"It's not funny," I snapped. "Willie, is that Merc still with us?"

He squinted into Andy's wing mirror. "Aye. I'll pull in here."

There was a row of parking bays on our right. The picnic site was deserted and the service station looked as if it had closed down years ago.

"As soon as I stop," he said, "everyone scatter."

"No, we should stay together," complained Andy.

The van skidded to a halt and we all bolted for the toilet block.

For a moment, there was no sign of the black Merc, then we heard it. All three of us tried our best to peer out through the hinge of the partly opened door. Four men, who looked more like gardeners than a bunch of Mafia hit-men, climbed out and strolled straight toward our position.

"Maybe they're just burstin' for a pee," said Andy in an anxious whisper.

"Where's Cat-Woman?" hissed Willie.

"Maybe she was just a random hitch-hiker after all," said Andy.

"Maybe she delivered us right to them," said Willie. "We don't really know who the fuck she is."

I wanted to snap back, but the truth was, I wasn't sure. She'd saved us before, but what if this was all part of the game? My gut told me she was on our side.

"She's saved our lives a few times already," I said. "Stay cool."

The four men were only twenty yards away now, so we backed further into the toilets and searched for an open window or a back door. Another way out.

"Here!" yelped Andy. He'd found the emergency exit, but was struggling with the release bar. The air was thick with the stench of carbolic soap and stale piss. It burned my nostrils. If this is how I was going to go, I'd rather have taken my chances outside.

We all pushed down on the metal release bar at the same time and the door swung outwards. Spilling out onto concrete beyond we tripped over a pile of beer crates and slammed into the bins.

Two men with black semi-automatics raised their aim.

Another two stepped out through the emergency exit behind us. They were carrying a pair of shovels.

One of the men outside, bald and much older than the rest said, "Don't move." His face was flecked with fairly recent cuts—like he'd just lost a fight with a rose bush.

We raised our hands above our heads.

"You were told to go back home, Mr Angus, but since you seem incapable of taking advice, we've decided to prolong your stay."

"How long?" said Andy, out of the blue, "because we've got

some gigs to play and–"

"Shut up," snapped the bald one.

The rest of the gang began laughing quietly, as if they knew something we didn't.

The bald one put his gun away and produced a thick metal bar from the inside of his jacket. He addressed the other men. "I'm not going to waste bullets on them." He pointed to the bushes behind us. "Make sure that their bodies are more than two feet below ground." I could tell he was nervous–always looking around, searching the bushes. Then it hit me. I recognised him.

"You were in the white sports car?" I muttered, still trying to make sense of it all. "You ended up on the barrier."

The bald man narrowed his eyes at me. "And this time you're not going to be so lucky."

CHAPTER FIFTEEN

I'd seen plenty of old cowboy films where they'd made a bunch of Mexicans dig their own graves before they blasted them, but this was just off the scale. We were in Italy, I'll give you that, but it was the twenty-first century, and we were literally yards from a service station. We'd been thrown some spades and told to dig a hole each, three feet deep by three feet wide, and seven feet long.

"Where's your fuckin' bodyguard?" whispered Willie, digging as slowly as he could.

I looked around us for any sign of Lorene but as soon as I did a henchman jabbed the muzzle of his automatic into my ribs.

"Keep digging!" he hissed hatefully.

Andy was trembling.

"Jesus," I pleaded. "I was only going to try and find my wife, see if we could patch things up."

This outburst only resulted in another jab in the ribs from the bald man.

Andy was digging way too fast.

"Slow down, you stupid ass," hissed Willie.

The bald man with the iron bar tapped it menacingly against the palm of his hand while the other three looked on impatiently. Only one of the remaining thugs held a semi-automatic, the rest had produced more iron bars, longer and heavier than the first. It seemed pretty obvious that they were going to beat us to death and then bury us.

"That will do," said the bald man.

Willie and I gave Andy a contemptuous stare.

"What?" complained Andy.

The bald man pointed at me. "Him first."

"Wait!" I yelped. "If you're going to kill me, at least tell me who gave you the order. Who stopped me from seeing Maria?"

The bald man hesitated, his heavy cudgel poised for the first strike. "Antonio Galdini is a very powerful man. You were very stupid Mr Angus. You should have remained in Glasgow."

"We can turn around. Go back home," I reasoned.

"It's too late for that," snapped the bald man. "You need to be removed from the equation." He nodded to the other thugs and they gathered round me while the one with the semi-automatic covered Willie and Andy.

I heard them grunt as they swung their weapons, so I braced. This was it.

Thud!

I opened one eye and saw the man with the gun shudder and then drop to his knees. A neat, black hole had appeared in the centre of his forehead.

There was a clang of iron as the others dropped their cudgels and reached for their guns, but Willie was too fast. He smashed his bony fist into the bald man's groin. There was another thud and the thug next to me crumpled. He tumbled straight into our neatly dug hole. He was still twitching when a spray of crimson jetted out of his throat.

Willie pulled the groaning bald man down with both hands and obliterated his nose with a head butt.

I jumped on the remaining thug as he pulled his gun.

He struggled as he fought to train his gun on me, but I twisted it out of his hand and performed a karate kick that caught him on the throat. He dropped, and my body snapped into an old stance I hadn't used in years.

Willie jumped away from the bald man, who was out cold and stared hard at me. "What the fuck did you just do?"

In the same instant, the man I'd downed, got up again. This time a forward kick mawashigeri caught him straight in the face.

Willie jumped on him and began pulverising the guy's skull, digging his heel into the wounded man's face until the guy's head looked like trampled fruit.

Andy shouted out at me, but it was too late. The messed up bald thug had gotten to his knees and thrown his iron bar. It glanced off my arm. Suddenly reanimated, I felt his knee catch my balls and I stopped breathing.

My vision was hazy. Someone leapt over me and I heard the iron bar hit the ground.

Lorene, in a move so fast it was hard to discern what she actually did, flicked her hands over the bald man's face. I saw his head whip round at a strange angle and heard a sickening crack. He dropped into another of the freshly dug holes, toppling over Andy.

"I think that one is dead, Willie," said Lorene.

Willie staggered back from the mess he'd made and rested his hands on his knees. "Fucker was going to kill us," he panted.

"Not any more, he's not," said Lorene. She was calm and focused.

Willie's attack had been utterly ferocious. The thug's head was flattened and his brains fanned out from his broken skull in a spray of pink and white lumps.

Lorene stooped down and scraped up one of his eyeballs.

"What are you doing?" I wheezed, in disgust.

She wrapped it in some cling film, pulled from a pouch on her hip, and slipped into her jacket. "The Mafia family houses are well guarded these days. They use retina recognition for entry."

"Where the fuck were you when we needed you?" hissed Willie. His anger now rounded on Lorene. "I thought you were supposed to protect us?"

"I did," she answered. "And just for future reference," she pointed straight at me, "I am only paid to protect him."

Lorene was already arranging the bodies in our newly dug pit. They flopped about, lifeless and limp; a bloody mêlée of twisted limbs and gore.

"I never knew you did that karate shit," said Andy.

"I don't," I replied.

"Yes, you do," said Lorene.

I stared at her, wishing she hadn't added her penny's worth. I'd never used karate since I was sixteen. All that stopped when I'd really hurt a kid at school. He'd lost an eye and I lost the will to ever use that stuff again. "Not any more."

Lorene seemed to sense my unease and squinted down at the bodies. "Bury them."

"But?" began Andy.

My mind was foggy. I couldn't understand why Lorene had left things so long before intervening. "You let us dig our own graves. I thought you'd buggered off," I protested.

"Well, I hadn't," she replied, "and thanks to your excellent question, your last dying request. I now know who and what we are dealing with."

"Another Galdini?" I said.

"Antonio Galdini, Franco's father, must have a contract out on you. He must be worried that you'll get to Maria and change her mind."

I wretched as I watched her kick some of Willie's victim's brains into the shallow grave. My legs were shaking and my mouth was so dry that my tongue stuck to the roof of my mouth. This wasn't out of disgust at what I was seeing, it was in disgust of what I'd just done. I'd broken a promise I'd made to myself long ago.

Lorene picked up a shovel. "I need you to help me bury them. Now."

We covered the bodies in a thick layer of dirt and trampled it down. Then we all picked up bundles of leaves and threw them over the site.

I trailed after Lorene, like a zombie, back to our van.

Just before we climbed in, however, Willie looked down at Andy's crotch. There was a dark patch around his groin.

"So, I pissed myself," said Andy. "I thought that was it. I thought I was going to die like a fuckin' Mexican bandit–behind a service station toilet."

"At least change yer fuckin' togs," moaned Willie.

Andy proceeded to step out of his jeans and pants while Lorene repacked her holdall and fixed her hair in the mirror.

I threw Andy a spare pair of jeans.

"Ta," he said, squinting at Lorene to see if she was looking.

She wasn't.

"Next time," said Willie, addressing Lorene, "don't leave it so long."

"I will do whatever it takes to keep him safe." She nodded at me.

"What should I do?" I asked. "What if I turn back now?"

Lorene looked me straight in the eye and said, "You'll still have a contract out on you. Nothing changes."

"So that means?" said Andy, sounding a bit more like his old self.

Lorene zipped her bag shut. "It means that you are all dead unless..." she paused, turning to face me, "unless Ian gets to

Maria first and manages to change her mind."

I could see that Willie was shaking. His knuckles were white and his face flushed. "What the hell have we got ourselves into?" He jumped out of the van and went back into the toilets.

"Look," I said, "I'm quite prepared to go the rest of the way on my own."

"That might be easier," added Lorene. "You will be less conspicuous if you travel alone."

"No, we should all keep going," said Andy, "they might pick us *all* off, no matter where we are. I'll feel better sticking with you," he nodded at Lorene, "and the karate kid, in there."

Willie emerged from the toilets and got up into the driver's seat. He shook his mobile phone. "Uncle Fred is going to meet us at the Redante," he explained. He started up the engine. "We are all in on this now."

"Shit," sighed Andy. "Do you think that's wise? Getting him involved?"

"Yes," said Willie, "after being forced to dig my own grave, this Galdini bunch are going to get a taste of Glaswegian 'hospitality'."

"When do you stop being my body guard?" I asked Lorene, suddenly very worried.

She gave me a churlish smile and said, "I stop when I'm told to stop."

CHAPTER SIXTEEN

Amazingly, I managed to get about four hours sleep on the last stretch of our trip to Rome. Driving in through the outskirts, we passed Olmetti and headed for the Castel Sant'Angelo.

"Are you sure you know where you're going?" asked Willie.

Andy checked his mobile and examined the minuscule map. "Just keep the river on your left-hand side. We should be on the 'Via Michelangelo' or something..."

I scanned the buildings for a road sign but couldn't see any. "So, Willie... your uncle?" I let the words hang in the musty air of the van for a moment. "Your Uncle Fred?"

"What about him?"

"Why is he coming over? Because, as far as I can see, he'll only make things worse."

"Bollocks," said Willie, still eyeing Lorene's tits in the rear-view mirror, "he wants to help. He'll beef up our protection."

Lorene, a wistful expression on her pretty face, continued to stare out of the window at the River Tevere.

"Earlier, you said that your wife gave you that key as a goodbye present," she mused.

"More like a 'get lost' present," chipped in Andy.

"Why would your wife give you a key to a casino she got on a beach ten years ago?" Lorene asked. "It's ridiculous."

"She didn't know what it was," I said. "It was symbolic."

Willie furrowed his freckled brow in thought, "I suppose there are three possibilities."

"Which are?" said Andy.

"One: Maria knows it's a key to a locker and wants Ian to find what's in there."

"Maybe she put a present in the locker to say sorry for being a slut for ten years," interrupted Andy.

Lorene looked puzzled.

"Ignore him," I said, "he's a dick-head."

"Or," continued Willie, two: the old man on the beach knew

who Maria was, and gave it to her on purpose before he died."

"But he died before he could tell her about it?" I asked.

Willie shrugged. "Or," he pressed on, "number three: it is just a complete coincidence that I have a key the exact same as yours and it was, as you say, 'symbolic'."

"I like the second option," said Lorene, "but there may be a fourth possibility. How do you know that your Uncle Fred isn't involved?"

Willie looked gobsmacked. "What?"

"What age is your uncle?" I asked.

"I don't know," snapped Willie. "Fifty or something."

"We should try your key too," said Andy. "Maybe it didn't expire after a week. Maybe Lorene's right. Your Uncle *is* a gangster."

"He's not any more," said Willie.

"Since when?" laughed Andy.

"Since he moved to Spain. He's just angry at someone trying to bump me off."

"How many times have you actually seen your Uncle Fred?" I asked.

"Loads... he helped my mum out when my dad..." Willie stopped talking as he turned into an underground car park.

"Tell him," prompted Andy.

"My dad was killed by a rival gang in the 80's. Uncle Fred gave us money for food and stuff–I owe him."

"Jesus," I sighed, "this stinks."

"What? The car park?" said Andy.

"No. His uncle. He must be in on this somehow. Lorene's right."

"Rubbish," snarled Willie. "He knows people. He might be able to help. Just remember, we were all involved in killing and burying four Galdini henchmen," reminded Willie.

I suddenly felt a wave of panic sweep over me.

"Shit," gasped Andy, "But no one knows that, right?"

Willie came to a slow stop. "Uncle Fred wanted to know everything."

"For fuck's sake," moaned Andy. "You didn't tell him?"

"Willie. Why did you…?"

"It was self defence," said Lorene. "And, I've been thinking," she added, "We should change vehicle."

"How are we going to do that?" blurted Willie.

Lorene dug into her holdall and produced a selection of passports.

"Now she's Mary Poppins," whispered Willie. "What else have you got in there?"

Lorene stifled a grin and said, "I carry what I need, no more. I will hire another van and bring it here in an hour."

"Let's go for a pint," said Andy.

"Nice one," said Willie.

I began to punch Maria's number into my mobile.

"Give me that!" said Lorene.

"But I want to try one more..."

She snatched the Nokia out of my hand and dismantled it in two seconds–removing the SIM card.

"Hey!" I protested.

"I am paid to look after you," she said, "so, you will come with me. You two," she flicked her slender fingers at Andy and Willie, "wait here, in the van. There will be no beer yet."

"Who says?" said Willie.

"I say," she replied, briskly. "If you want to live, do what you're told."

We all stared at each other, wide-eyed for a long moment before I said, "She's saved our lives twice."

"Three times," Lorene corrected.

Willie punched the side of the Transit van in frustration.

"Come on." Lorene took my hand and led me towards the exit like a two-year-old.

"Remember, don't let go mummy's hand," taunted Willie.

Self-consciously, I slipped my hand free of hers and tried to keep up.

"What if someone comes down here looking for us?" shouted Andy.

"Hide," Lorene shouted back, over her shoulder.

I could hear Willie moaning at Andy. "We're in fuckin' Rome, stuck in an underground car park, with nothing to drink."

Outside, behind the Piazza Cavour, in a narrow backstreet, Lorene found a small car rental company called, *Vichy Cars*. She went inside and hired a Mercedes van. It wouldn't be ready for another thirty minutes so we found a café opposite and ordered some food.

"Tell me again, why do you hang about with those two?" asked Lorene.

This was a good question. "I've known them since I was eighteen," I replied, unconvincingly.

"You would be much safer without them," she continued. "Let them play their precious music by themselves. Come back to Scotland with me. My job will be easier if you are far away from all this. I like you. I don't want to see you hurt."

I looked at her closely and realised that I was kidding myself. She was as close to Audrey Hepburn as anyone could ever be in looks–and probably in her late twenties. And there was me, convinced, for one fleeting moment, that she fancied me.

I watched Lorene sip her espresso and my thoughts drifted back to Willie and Andy. "I can't abandon my friends," I explained, "good or bad, they're all I have. And they've almost been killed because of me..."

"I am simply trying to increase your chances of survival," said Lorene. "If Willie's uncle faces up to the Sardinian Mafia on their own turf, he will die. It doesn't matter how resourceful he is in Glasgow. This is Italy – they'll torture him, then they will kill him."

"I need to find Maria," I whispered, anxiously. "I was crazy to let her go without a fight."

Lorene stared out into a street full of long shadows. "I hope you can win that fight, Ian. I hope you find your wife and get a chance to hear what she has to say."

"I need to go back to Dead Dog Beach," I said. "Something happened in that place and I missed it."

"You miss plenty."

She stared at me again over the rim of her coffee cup, and this time I got the feeling that she knew me. Somehow... from long ago.

"Have we ever met before?" I asked.

She smiled into her coffee. "Not really."

What was that supposed to mean?

"How far are we from the Redante?" I asked.

"Not that far," she said.

A small man with a stoop crossed the street outside—and my heart instantly sank. "That's Fred Marvin," I whispered. "I recognise his face from all the pictures in the papers."

Lorene nodded at another man who had just met up with Fred Marvin. Older and sallow skinned, he'd stepped out of a parked car.

"That's Antonio Galdini," whispered Lorene.

"The guy who has a—"

"—contract out on you? That's him."

I slid down a little further in my seat.

CHAPTER SEVENTEEN

Fred Marvin was tanned and bald apart from a laurel-shaped swish of grey that framed his perfectly polished dome. He had a kind smile that I imagined could switch quite effortlessly to an evil, malicious one—and he had the dented posture of a weasel.

"I told you he was involved in your mess," whispered Lorene.

"Willie asked him here, that's all," I whispered back.

"Antonio Galdini is a butcher," said Lorene. "No one can prove it, of course, but he is said to have murdered over two hundred opponents."

"Opponents?" I replied anxiously.

"Anyone who stands in his way. Anyone who dares to speak against him."

"So, you think Fred is mixed up with this guy? I mean, even before Willie's call."

Lorene gave me a look bordering on pity, like I had no clue about pretty much anything.

"Galdini once skinned a whole family alive for refusing to pay protection money. A baker from Napoli, who could hardly rub two euros together, was forced to watch his wife and kids..."

This was the first time I'd seen so much as a trace of emotion from Lorene.

"God... Lorene, why is my Maria mixed up with these people?" I looked closely at the two killers. They honestly seemed like a couple of old gents meeting up to put a bet on a horse, or maybe play some bowls.

"Maria was born into that life." Lorene suddenly nodded at a black saloon car parked a few yards away. "Look over there. In the shadows, next to a big roll-top bin."

I glanced over and saw two men wearing dark glasses. They shifted nervously and scanned the street as the two old gangsters chatted.

"Minders," whispered Lorene.

"Fred and Antonio..." I said, "look as if they know each other pretty well."

"Perhaps." She didn't sound convinced.

"Shit, they're coming into the café," I hissed.

"Kiss me," she said.

I stared at her in disbelief.

"Do it!"

The door of the café swung inward as I pressed my lips against hers.

The adrenaline-driven kiss seemed to last for an age, as Lorene wrapped her arms around me and teased the hair at the back of my neck. Her lips were full, soft and warm. I could taste a mixture of strawberry lipstick and coffee–I hated the stuff, but I didn't care. I hadn't kissed anyone like that for about ten years.

I squinted at Fred and Giorgio as they settled into a corner table. Their louts loitered outside, each of them with a hand tucked purposely into their designer jackets.

Lorene released me and began stroking my arm.

"Giggle, then get up and follow me outside," she whispered. "And don't look in their direction. Marvin might know what you look like. Let me do the talking."

When she giggled, and rose from the table, I forced a smile and, fixing an easy eye on the sway of her slender hips, I followed her out onto the street.

"Nous ne faisons pas assez l'amore," she said in a mischievous voice.

I had no idea what it meant, but it seemed to amuse the two guards, who smiled knowingly at each other.

Around a hundred feet away from the café I realised that we'd missed a real opportunity to eavesdrop on the two gangsters. "If we'd only waited a few more minutes we might have found out what this is all about," I complained.

Lorene stared up at me. "You did well. You have some acting skills and you can fight, but what is my primary directive?"

I wanted to say, 'To tease me and test my resolve', but instead, I said, "to protect me."

"That is correct," she said, firmly. Lorene pulled me into the next alleyway. "But let's get one thing straight. The next time I have to kiss you, keep your bloody tongue to yourself."

"I didn't," I lied. "I just thought... You're French."

She smiled and shook her head. "Next time you try a French kiss, I will return the favour with a Glaswegian one. Understood?"

"Fine," I said, my face flushing. All my pathetic hopes, and now obvious misinterpretations, drifting away. I felt empty inside.

She marched out of the alley and onward towards the car-hire office.

"Surely, you wouldn't harm the merchandise, Lorene," I called after her.

She stopped beside a brand new, white van and said, in a French accent dripping with sex, "My contract states that I only need to keep you alive for the next three days."

I felt a flood of anxiety. "What do you mean? Why only three days?" I caught her by the shoulder but saw that the guy from the car hire office was staring at me, as if I was some kind of wife-beater. "You said you would stay with me until I was safe or..."

"Everything okay?" he asked, forcefully.

Lorene smiled sweetly, like a battered wife who still wanted to protect her man, and took the keys from his hand.

The car hire guy eyed me suspiciously as we checked for any previous damage to the vehicle. "Here's my number," he said to Lorene, rather than to me, "should you need any assistance."

"She'll be fine," I said. He'd managed to piss me off in five seconds, and I now felt that I had to play up to his expectations. "Won't you, dear?"

Lorene blew my unwanted cover just as quickly by simply saying, "Fuck off, and get in."

The man hesitated, his unsure eyes flicking between us.

I 'got in', before he could say anything and we drove to the underground car park in silence.

Inside, on the gloomy concrete ramp that led back down to Andy and Willie, I repeated my question, "Why three days?"

She shrugged, her arms outstretched, gripping a steering wheel that was much too big for her. "I'm guessing they think you'll be irrelevant after your wife is married."

"Maria, getting married–it doesn't even sound right."

"Sorry, but you were never properly married the first place."

"And you really don't know who is paying you?" I pressed.

"I never do," she replied. "I told you. I prefer it that way."

Lorene came to a stop before we reached the old van. "What made you stop karate, give up your skills?"

My mouth went dry. I didn't really want to talk about it. I could see our Transit. The back doors were open and Willie was sitting on the sill strumming my Les Paul. Andy was tapping out a rhythm on the blue paintwork of one of the back doors. "I hurt someone in a fight. He was a bully and I used my skills in the wrong kind of way."

"And?" She pressed.

"And I blinded him."

There was an eerie silence as our new white van coasted to a stop.

"Took your bloody time, didn't you?" said Andy.

My Les Paul was a flame-top maple, 59 reissue–Gary Moore style. I hated anyone else touching it. Willie bloody knew that.

"Your strings are rusted to fuck," he complained.

"Put it away, Willie. If I so much as farted on your bass, you'd kick my arse up my back for a hump."

"So, go for it!" he said. "Oh, right enough," he added, "I forgot about your super skills." He nodded at Lorene. "And you have back up."

Lorene shook her head at him dismissively. "Just move all that," she pointed at our band gear, "into that." She pointed at the new van, a white Merc, and went to collect her holdall.

In seconds, however, she was racing back towards us. "Who's been through my things?"

Willie and Andy looked like a couple of schoolboys who'd just been caught cracking one off in the toilets. They began nodding at each other, as if to say 'you go first'.

"Fuck's sake," I moaned, "did you touch her guns and shit?"

"My guns are fine," snapped Lorene.

I was puzzled. "So what …?" Then it dawned on me. I glanced at them and said, "You didn't …?"

"What?" said Willie, half-laughing.

Lorene stared at me. "They've been rummaging through my underwear."

"I was only looking for something to blow my nose on," mumbled Andy.

"You are a couple of dirty bastards!" she yelled.

Willie smirked as he took hold of a four-by-twelve speaker cabinet. "Nice scanties," he confided to me, as we grunted and panted in the echoed confines of the parking lot.

"You're nothin' but a couple of misogynistic bastards stuck in the 70's."

Willie and Andy both looked at me for a second before Andy said, "And you're not?"

"You changing sides, pal?" added Willie. "Too loved up to be one of the boys anymore?" He winked at Lorene, who looked ready to punch his face in.

I took a deep breath before saying, "We met your nice, old Uncle Fred."

"What?" said Andy, overhearing. "He's here already?"

"He was talking, all buddy-buddy, to that Mafia boss Lorene told us about–Antonio Galdini."

"I told you he would sort this out," said Willie.

"Jesus, Willie, don't you remember what that bald bastard said when he was about to club us to death and bury us alive?" I pressed.

"He basically said that he worked for Galdini," said Andy. "Antonio Galdini."

Willie turned to Lorene. "What happened?"

Lorene, her expression still as black as thunder, said, "It looks like your uncle is on the same side as the Galdini family. The very people who were going to kill you."

Willie's complexion turned the colour of boiled shite. "But we're supposed to meet him in twenty minutes at the casino."

CHAPTER EIGHTEEN

The Redante Casino had a neoclassic, white-painted façade with intricate balustrades and balconies that oozed 'old money'. The kind of money that comes from generations of successful speculation or carefully concealed crime.

"There's no such thing as clean money," said Andy, as if he'd just read my mind.

"You can say that again," added Lorene.

The Redante was massive. Twin-towered and expansive, an array of international flags hung over its opulent entranceway like some giant headdress.

"Can you see him?" asked Andy.

"No," said Willie, "and I'm not sure I want to now."

"You're the one who invited him," I said.

Willie gave me a dagger of a glance and then went back to chewing his nails. "Maybe he had some other business with Galdini."

"And maybe I've got a twelve-inch cock," said Andy.

Lorene glanced down. "Maybe four."

I chuckled nervously.

Willie remained dead-pan.

"What's the worst that can happen?" continued Andy.

"Let me see," I said. "We all go over and greet Willie's favourite uncle, and every last one of us is mown down in a hail of bullets. Then they pick through our lukewarm corpses until they find the key."

Willie pulled into a parking space at the side of the casino and we all got out.

"You think that's it?" asked Lorene. "You think the only reason he came here is for some key that your wife, Maria, had round her neck for ten years? Why didn't he just take it from her, in Glasgow?"

We were standing behind a neatly cut hedge about two hundred yards from the casino entrance.

"What exactly did you say to your Uncle Fred when you phoned him?" I asked.

Willie closed his eyes in thought. "I'm not sure. Something like: we've been made to dig our own graves by a bunch of Mafia freaks in Italy, so we might need some help."

"So you didn't say anything about a key?" I pressed.

"Of course I did," said Willie, irritably. "I told him that you had a key just like the one he gave me on his stag night. And I think I told him that I still had mine and a little about the dead dog bit in Sardinia."

"Brilliant!" I snapped. "Instead of putting them off our trail, we're worse off than ever."

Willie pointed a long, skinny finger at my face. "You didn't say the key bit was a fuckin' secret!"

"Look," said Lorene, "we have a few options: walk straight over there and see what happens, or we can stay low, basically hide for three days."

"Why three days?" asked Willie.

"Oh yeah," I piped up, "Lorene told me that I only have her services for three days."

"After which …?" said Andy.

Lorene and I both shrugged at the same time.

"I say we all shack up in some hotel room and get comfy," said Andy, leering at Lorene's ass.

"If you look at my ass one more time, I'll knock your eye out," she snapped.

"It's not my fault that you've got a great ass," complained Andy.

"Look," I interrupted, "I'm betting that Willie will be in the 'bad books' if Uncle Fred comes all this way and then he doesn't even bother to turn up."

"Shit," said Willie.

"So," continued Lorene, still sounding angry, "here's what we have to do," she looked at me, "if you insist on being 'one of the boys' with these two degenerates …?"

I gave a half-hearted nod.

"We split into two groups. Randy Andy and Willie go meet with the Glasgow gangster and find out if Maria's key still opens a locker... We stay back and observe."

"He knows that Ian is with us," complained Willie.

"I'm not convinced he knows what Ian looks like," said Lorene. "You could say that Ian wasn't well, or that he had a hangover."

"Shit," said Willie, "there he is."

For the second time that day I saw Willie's Uncle Fred, one of Glasgow's most notorious gangland bosses. His face was pale, gaunt and pitted.

"He's by himself," whispered Willie.

"So, go," urged Lorene.

Reluctantly, Willie and Andy shuffled across the manicured gardens towards the entrance of the Redante.

Lorene and myself waited and watched.

Fred Marvin waved at Willie and smiled.

"Look. There, to the left of Fred," said Lorene, "it's the two gangsters we saw at the café."

Sure enough, as soon as Willie and Andy said their hellos and went inside, the two gangsters followed.

"Let's go shadow," said Lorene.

Again, adopting the role of a love-struck couple, we strolled up to the casino foyer and paid our entrance fee.

"A hundred euros each?" I squawked.

"It's fine," murmured Lorene. "I'll put it down as part of my expenses."

She paid up and we went in.

As soon as we walked through the main doors of the gaming room, I saw Willie and Andy being led round by Fred Marvin. He looked serious as Willie chatted to him. Andy nodded every so often, as if to emphasise a point, but trailed a good three yards behind them.

Inside, the Redante was as elegant as its grand façade. American roulette tables were set at each corner of the expansive hall while the main space was packed with blackjack tables, poker tables and slot machines of every colour and size imaginable.

Usherettes with skirts short enough to make your granny faint mingled with the gamblers while beefy heavies remained close to the walls, not too conspicuous, but on hand if needed. They all wore neatly pressed suits, black and cut from the finest cloth.

The clientele was around eighty percent male but a few of the women present seemed to be the most passionate players of all. Often thumping a table in frustration with one hand while balancing a cocktail in the other, they argued and babbled their misgivings.

Music filtered in from another set of doors to the back of the hall where a sign flashed the name of the act on stage at any given time. Croupiers cut decks and fanned out cards on green, baize tables while keeping a watchful eye out for any trickery or sleight of hand.

"Where are they?" said Lorene in an urgent whisper.

I'd lost sight of them too. "Damn... They were over by that roulette wheel a second ago."

I felt a tap on the shoulder.

"Mr Angus?"

Lorene let out a cry as a big guy pressed a piece of gauze over her mouth and a further four pulled her behind a thick curtain.

I suddenly stood alone, barely fifty yards from the front door, my legs practically buckling with shock. Everyone else was so engrossed in betting their fortunes away that the whole incident had passed unnoticed.

I felt my arms being grabbed and almost drew on my old skills again. I'd broken my duck and might have been able to slip free, but I decided it would be better to go along. See where they'd taken Lorene.

"The boss would like a word," said one of the two men holding me. He was tall and thin, yet very strong. I could feel his vice-like grip beginning to cut off the blood supply in my arm. "Where is my friend?"

"Safely disarmed," said the other man, shorter and portlier. He had designer stubble and a very pronounced widow's peak.

"Who... who is the boss, again?" I asked, pathetically, as I was led behind a thick velvet curtain.

The smaller man laughed and said, "Someone you don't want to fuck with."

A dark corridor and two rooms later, I was led into a large office, much less imposing than I'd expected.

I almost choked when I saw who was sitting behind the austere, mahogany desk.

CHAPTER NINETEEN

"You!" I blurted. I recognized his smile, the one that meant business. It was Carlos Azuni–the sleek Italian bastard who'd walked into my house the night Maria walked out. He was sitting back in a padded, leather chair looking, for all the world, like a Mafia boss.

"Mr Angus," he began, "what was the last thing I said to you?"

I thought back to the white removals van parked outside my house, stuffed full of our furniture. I thought about Andy driving home from his gig half-pissed and, of course, about 'the warning' this man had given us. "You said something about not following you or–"

"Or you would be killed," said one of Azuni's henchmen.

I flashed him a puzzled glance before I said, "Yes, but I didn't think you had actually meant it." Inside, however, I knew fine-well that he had.

"Really?" said Azuni, a trace of disappointment on his handsome face. "I must be losing my touch."

"Look, Mr Azuni, where is Lorene? This is my fault. You didn't have to be so rough with her."

"Ah," he said, "this is very interesting. Rather than ask about the whereabouts and, indeed, safety of your wife, Maria, you concern yourself with the predicament of a ruthless assassin."

"I... You..." I said, floundering.

His smile widened as he waved away his henchmen.

Once the room had cleared his expression hardened. "You disobeyed me."

My gut twisted as fear and fury jostled for first place. "What is this all about? Why do I even need an assassin to protect me? What are you to Maria?" I stood up. "Where is she?"

He played with a tuft of beard, directly beneath his lower lip, moving his forefinger in little circles. "So what do you want first: information about Maria, or information about Lorene Duvall?"

He shook his head. "No need to answer, your pupils dilated when I mentioned Lorene."

"They did not," I protested.

"Lorene," he pressed on, "is top-drawer." He caught my expression and added, "In more ways than one."

"*You* managed to subdue her," I said.

"With five men and a dose of chloroform," he said. "And that was only because we had the element of surprise."

"What will you do with her?" I asked.

He inhaled and exhaled slowly before saying, "That all depends on you."

"And Maria?" I asked.

"Your ex-wife is not to be disturbed."

"For all I know you may have chloroformed her too."

Carlos Azuni straightened his tie and then began tapping his fingers on the mahogany table. "The thing is... I'm now tempted to let you go on your way…see who's paying Lorene. Find out why the Glasgow gangster, Fred Marvin, is here."

I felt my temper rise again, my impatience growing by the second.

"Please tell me what you know."

"I can't. If I did, I would soon be digging my own grave."

He bit down a malicious grin.

"So it was you who set those gangsters on us," I said.

"No," he said, quite simply, "it was Antonio Galdini. But it was me who dug them up and got rid of the evidence. Galdini is not a happy man just now. Some of his men have gone missing."

"What about the white sports car back in Leon?"

"The one Lorene dealt with?" said Azuni. "Again, Galdini."

"So, you work for Galdini?" I pressed.

Azuni smirked. "Absolutely not. But I know that he sees you as a threat."

"Why? I play in a band."

"You are also connected to Maria, and that makes him nervous."

"What can I possibly do to him?" I whined.

"More than you think," he answered.

"Lorene told us that Antonio Galdini will take this place over when Maria…" I didn't even want to say it, "joins Franco

Galdini, and brings the two families together."

He stared at me for a long moment, before saying, "She did, did she?"

"Seems to me that you might not like that." I whispered nervously.

Carlos Azuni snapped a pencil he was playing with and stared straight at me. "Here's what's going to happen."

I braced.

"I'm going to let you see Maria one more time."

"Where?"

"She is already in Sardinia with Franco."

My heart sank. "So you want things to stay the same–the family dynamics…"

"They can't," he hissed, "But you might be able to stop the union. Make her see sense."

"So, you've tried?" I could tell by his face that he had. "But you work for the Savianos. If they ever found out you were–"

"Enough!" His eyes narrowed. "I cannot be seen to interrupt destiny." He looked about nervously. "You might just make it to Sardinia if Miss Duval is with you."

"So you won't kill me then?" I asked.

He knocked three times on the desk, and the door behind me opened. Four heavies shuffled in, two either side of a very groggy-looking Lorene.

"Miss Duvall. How nice to see you again."

Lorene coughed and shook a strand of hair from her eyes. "Carlos."

Carlos Azuni smiled. "Here's what will happen from now on." He pointed to me, "Mr Angus will continue on his pilgrimage to Sardinia, only because I'm interested to see what follows in his wake."

Lorene looked surprised.

"What are you playing at, Carlos?" said Lorene.

"Knowledge is power, Lorene. You know that."

"You are in charge of protection for the Saviano family. I know that much," she said, defiantly.

"For now," I added, under my breath.

"You!" snapped Azuni. His hateful expression quickly softened as he stood up and straightened his black tie. "The less you know, the more chance you have of survival."

He paused and raised a questioning finger. "Why is the Scottish gangster here?"

"For additional protection," I said quickly.

Lorene flashed me a worried glance.

Azuni laughed. "Now that's a bit of a slap on the face, isn't it, Lorene?"

We were frogmarched along another corridor until we reached a security room packed with monitors.

"Where did Mr Angus' friends go?" asked Azuni.

Three of the heavies scanned the screens before one pointed. "There, to the lockers."

"Willie … our bass-player," I began, "his uncle took him here for a stag night, gave him a private room." I explained.

I could see that Lorene was regaining her strength. Her eyes sharpened as she freed an arm.

Azuni spun round. "Let her go."

The heavies backed away from her, like she was a cobra.

"So why did you split up?" asked Azuni.

"They wanted to play the machines," explained Lorene.

Azuni shook his head.

"So?" I mused, trying to change the subject, "the Galdinis might change this place when they take over."

Seemingly annoyed by the mere mention of the word 'Galdini', Azuni pushed me back against the wall.

In the same instant, Lorene peeled Azuni's fingers from my chest like they were Velcro, flipped him, and forced him to the floor. She slipped a gun from his inside pocket and brought it up against his head.

The heavies moved in but Azuni shouted, "Stay back!"

Lorene spoke calmly, "Just let us go on our way with our friends and we will do what you say."

"I should have known better," sighed Azuni.

"Deal?" pressed Lorene, forcing the muzzle of the gun harder against Azuni's head.

"Deal!" spat Azuni.

Lorene nodded to a second door behind Azuni and I slid away from the wall. Lorene followed, the gun still pointed at Azuni. "One more thing," she said.

"What?" snapped Azuni.

"Call an ambulance."

"Why?" asked Azuni.

In a blur, Lorene smacked the butt of the gun into the face of the heavy next to Azuni, grabbed the TASER from his belt, and discharged it into his groin. "Because this pervert is going to need one."

The heavy dropped and shuddered like an eel on the floor, his nose spattered across his face.

"If he behaved dishonourably, he deserved that, but you can't open that door… unless you have clearance." Azuni nodded at a scanner on the wall.

Lorene removed a small plastic bag from the lining of her jacket–and pulled out a bloody eyeball like it was a hotel key.

The henchmen all took a synchronised step back as she held it up to the retina scanner.

The door whooshed open.

Carlos Azuni reeled back. "Who? What was that?"

"That belonged to a Galdini henchman," said Lorene, "If he had access, it looks like things are going to change here quicker than you think."

We stepped out amongst the flashing lights of the casino slot machines; bells ringing, coins clattering, a throng of people yelping and cursing.

"What did that guy do to you?" I called after her.

"He took advantage of a lady," she snapped over her shoulder, marching swiftly towards the exit.

"Ian!"

I turned to see Andy, grinning like a kid, waving a fistful of yellow chips. "It's brilliant in here, isn't it?"

CHAPTER TWENTY

"We're going right now, Andy," I panted.

"But I need to cash in my chips," he complained.

I stopped and looked back into the main hall of the casino, the irony of his words floating round in my head. "Forget it. Where's Willie?"

"There!" said Andy in an anxious voice, pointing up to the left corner of the foyer.

Willie and his Uncle Fred were winding their way down the most luxurious spiral staircase I'd ever seen. They were following an extremely glamorous usherette. She wore a black pencil skirt and a short, neatly-fitting jacket. Willie's eyes were, predictably, locked onto her derrière.

Lorene had the gun tucked into the back of her black jeans, the grip cutely concealed by her navy cashmere jacket. On seeing Fred, her right hand whisked round her back and hovered over the butt of the gun.

I could tell that Andy was about to have a strop. His face had reddened and he had planted himself, like a huffy child, about ten yards from the cashier's desk.

Willie suddenly saw us and waved a sheet of paper like he was doing semaphore, an excited expression lighting up his face.

"It was very stupid of us to let Willie and his uncle take the key," whispered Lorene. "I apologize for my lack of professionalism."

"We did it for Willie," I reminded.

Andy began walking toward the cashier.

"I told you, no!" I warned.

Andy froze and cursed. "For fuck's sake, Ian. I won two grand!"

"This is my Uncle Fred," said Willie, his voice uncharacteristically posh.

"Willie! Tell Ian," Andy pleaded.

Fred, who now had a briefcase chained to his left hand

presented me with his right, so I shook it. His skin was as rough as sandpaper.

"We should go," he told Andy.

Andy looked dumfounded. "What is going on?"

As Fred and Willie marched towards us, I noticed that his Uncle's nails were bitten down to the quick. He flashed a mouthful of unnaturally white caps and said, "Ian... Willie has told me so much about you." He sounded like a Member of Parliament rather than an infamous hood. Like a posh Stanley Baxter.

"Can we all go outside and talk?"

Fred nodded. "It might be best."

His quick compliance confused me a little.

"Come, Mr Marvin," said Lorene. She pointed at Andy and Willie in turn before jerking her thumb over her shoulder.

Lorene stormed out of the casino and we all followed.

I glanced about nervously, half-expecting one of Azuni's heavies to burst out of the doors behind us.

The evening sun was still warm and there was an aroma of fresh bread and coffee filtering into the gardens of the Piazza Cavour. Our new van was less than a hundred yards away and we felt safe enough to stop and talk. We all sat down on some wrought-iron benches.

Slightly bewildered looking, Fred Marvin plonked himself down on a park bench beside Willie and caught my eye. "Why the sharp exit, son?"

"I could ask you the same thing," interrupted Lorene. "First things first: why did you have a meeting with Antonio Galdini this morning?"

Fred looked stunned. "So you were spying on me?"

"No," I interjected, "you both literally walked into our café. It was a kind of coincidence, but..."

Willie had a face like a monkey's arse, all red and puffy. "We don't want to be nosy, your business is your business, Uncle Fred, but..."

"But you're going to be nosy anyway, Willie?" finished Fred. "I know Antonio from years back. He has family in Glasgow and we've done a bit of business now and again."

"But Uncle Fred," said Willie, "it was Galdini, at least some of his men, that were going to kill us. That's why I phoned you."

"And that's why I went straight to him first. Antonio Galdini understands family. He said he would call his men off if you came back to Glasgow with me," said Fred. "Things are complicated down here just now. There are a lot of changes in the air. Best not to get involved."

Andy was still clutching his yellow chips from the casino.

"What's in the briefcase?" asked Lorene.

"Just something I left behind the last time I was here with Willie," he replied.

"What do you know about my Maria?" I asked.

Fred leaned back and looked up at the tree tops. Four or five green parrots were squawking loudly above our heads. "Your wife was only out on loan, son," he said. "She was always going to go back home."

Lorene scanned the gardens as Fred talked.

"Maria is the daughter of Charles Saviano."

"Told you," snapped Andy.

"Charles is just out of prison after ten years... He's hiding somewhere in Sardinia, but he's waiting for her promise to be fulfilled. Maria promised that she would marry into the Galdini family once he was released from prison."

"Why?" I barked. "She's married to me."

"Not technically," said Fred.

I felt my stomach churn. "But?"

"Your wedding in Sardinia was a sham," said Fred, "False priest, false papers…the guests were mostly actors. It was a way of keeping Maria safe, well away from the place until Charles and Franco did their time."

"Galdini's son was in prison too?" asked Willie.

"There was a lot of tit for tat stuff going on back then," explained Fred.

My throat had locked up. My brain was sprinting but going nowhere.

"Prison is one of the easiest places to make a hit. Murderers already in place, weapons not a problem," said Fred. "So they made a truce. Charles and Franco would both be safe in prison until they did their time. Maria, rather than do 'God knows what' for ten years in Sardinia would be allowed to have a life, but somewhere far away with a 'stooge'.

"A stooge?" I repeated. "This is a pile of crap, and you know it. I don't care who you are..."

Willie widened his eyes in warning, but Fred just shrugged. "I would be pissed off too if I were you. But that's the truth. Maria will marry Franco Galdini in three days and seal the pact made by their parents ten years ago. It will stop a feud and combine all the wealth and land they own in one fell swoop."

"And what about me?" I was shaking.

"A loose end? A threat to the pact? I'm not sure how you've managed to get as far as you have." Fred smiled admiringly at me.

We all looked at Lorene. I wanted to say something—anything—but every word I had felt wrong.

"What about the key?" she asked.

"The key," said Willie, "I'd almost forgotten." He dug deep into his pocket and produced the brass key. "It was a locker key, right enough, but..."

Fred nodded. "When we opened the locker, it was empty, son."

I was still fuming, trembling with a mixture of shock and rage.

"I suppose you thought the locker contained the location of the four judges?" said Fred. "Lucky it was empty, if you ask me. Everyone would want you dead then. That's the one piece of information that would destroy both families for good."

I sighed and said, "So this whole trip to Rome was a waste of time?"

Fred smiled, still clutching his case like a new-born. "Come home with me, son—while you still can."

I stared at Fred. "No. You better tell Galdini that we are carrying on." I wasn't sure I meant what I was saying, but I carried on anyway. "Between now and reaching Sardinia, we're going to work this whole thing out."

Fred stared down at his feet and shook his head. "You will never make it to Sardinia."

"I have to see if Maria will come back." I said this without really feeling it. In fact, it felt like I was betraying Lorene.

Lorene issued a little sigh.

Fred looked straight into my eyes. It felt as though a ghostly hand had reached inside my ribcage and wrenched out my heart. In that instant, I could suddenly see the monster that lay behind the polite voice and the galling snobbery. "You'll do what your fucking told."

CHAPTER TWENTY-ONE

Willie made to get up from the bench but Lorene waved a finger of warning without taking her eyes off Fred. She calmly rested her hand on Fred's shoulder, like she was ordering coffee, not challenging a gangster. "We are going to continue on our journey, Mr Marvin."

Fred stood up, brushing Lorene's hand away. "Are you telling me that someone has ordered you to continue?"

"I am telling you nothing," said Lorene. "I am here to protect Ian—no matter where he decides to go."

"Look!" snapped Fred, impatiently.

She motioned me to follow her.

"Ian," said Willie, almost in tears, "What are you doing? Uncle Fred has come all this way—you should do what he says."

"Galdini told him to come, not you. There is more to this than meets the eye," said Lorene, glancing down at the briefcase.

"Look!" I pointed towards the casino. Three of Azuni's heavies had strolled into the Piazza Cavour.

"We should go," said Lorene.

Fred looked anxious.

Andy and Willie got up and followed us into the bushes.

A bullet screamed past my head and thudded into an acacia tree.

"Shit!" snapped Fred. "They said they would hold off!"

Still running, Lorene shouted over her shoulder, "Those guys aren't Galdini's men."

"Who are they?" yelled Fred.

His question went unanswered as we raced blindly through the shrubs and bushes. A thorny vine clawed at my arm and I cursed as we all spilled into a clearing.

"It's a dead end!" yelled Willie.

Ten feet away, a high fence barred our way.

"Now what?" wailed Andy.

"We stand and fight," said Lorene.

"They've got fuckin' guns!" hissed Willie.

Fred stared hard at Lorene. "Do you have another gun?"

"No, and I wouldn't give you it if I had." She pulled me close and said, "You stay with me. You two..." she pointed at Andy and Willie, "Get under that tree."

Confused, I followed Lorene. Andy and Willie disappeared from sight.

"You!" said Lorene. I watched Lorene point her gun at Fred. "Get your back against that fence. You're the bait."

I could hear Willie. "For the love of fuck, what is she doing?" His voice was a full octave higher than usual.

Lorene prodded Fred with the muzzle of the gun until his shoulders bounced off the high, wire-mesh fence. It rattled loudly.

"Stay," she snapped, pulling me back behind a bush.

Moments later the first of the heavies thundered into the clearing. "Don't move!"

I held my breath.

Fred raised a hand in surrender, the other still clutched his case.

Two more heavies, one of whom I recognised as the guy Lorene had tasered in Azuni's office, joined the first.

"Where are the rest of them?" he grunted.

"Over the fence," lied Fred. "I couldn't make it."

The heavy threw a disbelieving glance at the top of the wire before turning his gun a full ninety degrees for a kill shot.

"Wait here," she whispered before spinning out from behind the tree. She caught the man's wrist. Twisting the gun from his hand she dropped him with a back-heeled kick which caught him behind the knee. Lorene pointed his gun and her own at the other two heavies.

The man she'd just floored tried to get up, so I ran out from cover and nailed him with a swift kick to the side of his head. He fell, unconscious, in a heap at Fred's feet.

"Not Bad, son," said Fred, giving me a curious glance.

My heart was pounding. I didn't really think I would remember anything from all that time ago, but all the moves were still there.

"Ian, bring the guys out," she said.

Willie joined his Uncle but exhaled in disbelief at Andy.

"Have you pished yourself again?"

"Fuck off," snapped Andy.

Lorene threw me one of the guns, which I caught like a hot potato.

"Hold it and point it at him," she said, nodding at the taller of the two heavies.

"That's twice that bitch has taken Giorgio out in an hour," said the guy I was covering.

"Giorgio?" I whispered, thinking back to the guy Lorene TASERED.

The smaller of the two was easing his hand towards his belt but Lorene flicked a broken branch up from the ground with her shoe. It smacked into his face and he dropped with a thud at the taller man's feet.

The remaining heavy raised his hands a little higher, his mouth hanging open in surprise.

"I'm not going to kill you because Azuni let us walk," said Lorene. "What I don't understand, is why you fired at us a moment ago."

The tall thug was staring over Lorene's shoulder at Fred. "We were firing at him."

Fred shifted nervously.

"Why?" pressed Lorene.

The tall thug spat at Fred's feet. "He works for Galdini. He came to the casino last year and emptied one of our safes. One hundred thousand euros. We only found out once he'd left. Galdini sent us a note to say thank you for the money. So, when we checked the video tape and saw him take that case from one of our lockers..."

I stared at Fred, a horrible feeling of dread washing over me.

"Winnings that were owed to Antonio Galdini," he snapped.

"Carlos says that you stole it!" snapped the remaining thug.

Fred moved away from the fence. "Give me your gun, Ian, and I'll drop this one."

He snapped his fingers at me but I knew by Lorene's glance to hold off.

Lorene shook her head mournfully. "You used your own nephew to get back in the casino and take what you wanted."

"It was Galdini or Carlos Azuni?" said Fred. He stared at the tall thug. "I figured the risk was greater from Galdini."

"You figured wrong," said the tall thug. "You and him," he pointed to Willie. "Neither of you will make it out of Rome alive."

Willie suddenly turned the colour of boiled shite. "Fuck."

"Did you know about this, Willie?" I bleated.

"No!" he protested.

"What? Your Uncle Fred robs the place while you are there and you know nothing?"

"I promise," said Willie.

"Here's what's going to happen," said Lorene. "You're going to tell Carlos that we will continue on to Sardinia. If we make it there, and he leaves us alone for the next three days, we will make sure he gets his hundred thousand back."

The thug looked disbelievingly at her before giving a reluctant shrug.

The other two thugs were beginning to come round.

Lorene told us to get going, but before she left the clearing she reached down and unclipped the TASER from the belt of the heavy she'd dropped once already in Azuni's office. She smiled as he opened his eyes, held the TASER to his balls–and fired.

There was a high-pitched scream and then he passed out again, his body still twitching involuntarily, his piss forming a puddle around his crotch.

We followed her out of the gardens and back to the van.

"What the hell are you doing?" panted Fred.

"Saving your life," she answered, swinging the door of the van open.

Willie got behind the wheel as we all packed ourselves into the new white van.

"What about Galdini?" asked Fred. "I need to give him this money and go straight back to Glasgow or he'll kill me and these boys."

Lorene handed Fred a mobile. "You're going to call him and tell him that you think you know where the coordinates are to the four judges."

"Fuck off! That's an instant death sentence," gasped Fred.

"But Ian's key opened an empty locker," said Willie. He gave the key back to me.

"He doesn't know that," said Lorene. "Tell him that the coordinates weren't in the locker but instructions on how to find them were."

I looked into Lorene's eyes–efficient, ruthless, always three steps ahead. I didn't know whether I loved her or feared her. Maybe both.

Fred took the phone and began to dial. "He won't believe me."

"Make him believe you," snapped Lorene.

We drove out of the car park and pulled the visors down against the low winter sun.

I waited to see what Fred would say.

"Hello. No... I..." He cupped the phone and gave Lorene a pleading stare.

She signalled him to continue by rotating her fore-fingers over each other.

"We have some information about the c ... co-ordinates," he stuttered. "Yes, I have the money but I want to make sure you are safe first. I need to keep going with the stooge a little longer."

There was a pause and then Fred clicked the mobile shut. "He says, either way, we are all dead meat."

Willie rolled his eyes. "Well that went fucking well. Not!"

I knew Galdini wouldn't fall for it, but it was worth a try.

"We are still alive," said Lorene.

"Not for long," said Fred.

Willie kept glancing at his Uncle Fred as we drove past a sign for Civitavecchia, the ferry port that would take us to Sardinia.

"Why didn't you tell me about the money, Uncle Fred?"

"My business is my business," he snapped.

Andy was rummaging about in his holdall, seemingly nonplussed. He pulled out the bundle of postcards. "All we have to do is figure out what Maria is trying to tell you in these postcards."

"She just wants Ian to know he's a fanny," said Willie. "Something we all know already."

"Speaking of which," I said, "tell us about that band you were in a few years ago."

Willie gave me a wicked stare.

"What were they called again?"

"Wren Pussy," said Andy.

Willie switched his nasty look to Andy.

I couldn't help myself. "I heard you were really tight."

"Can't get tighter than a wren's pussy," Andy chuckled.

Willie slowed a little for traffic. "Fuck off!"

Andy motioned a karate chop with his right hand. "We didn't know about the Karate Kid moves, though–did we, Ian?"

It was always funny how Andy could turn the tables on me. Even when we'd cornered Willie for once. He always preferred taking the piss out of me.

It was probably a safer bet, I decided.

CHAPTER TWENTY-TWO

I thought Civitavecchia was a pretty drab-looking port. A selection of container ships, oil storage tanks and rusty cranes lined a dockside that seemed devoid of any human life. The gargantuan cruise ship that dominated the skyline, however, hinted at an alien invasion of some kind.

"Americans," muttered Lorene, as if she'd just said the word, 'rats'. "They bus them back and forth to the Colosseum."

Our queue, the one for the Olbia ferry, was further along the waterfront, and at least a mile long.

As we came to a halt behind a tanker marked, 'Grazie per l'olio d'oliva', I saw Andy ping the elastic band from the bundle of postcards. He slid one free.

"What's this shite?" Fred stared down at the bundle. He'd unbuttoned his shirt, which had a collar of Harry Hill proportions, and exposed a grey tangle of wiry chest hair. The obligatory gold medallion lay somewhere in the hoary thicket, a hint of twenty-four-carat bling winking through the undergrowth.

"That Azuni guy," began Andy, "the one who runs the casino, turned up at Ian's house the night Maria left..."

"You mean the one that told his men to shoot me?" said Fred.

"Yes. Well," said Andy, "it was him that gave us these cards."

"Maria wrote a postcard to her friend, Julie, every time we went on holiday," I explained.

"You were right the first time, Uncle Fred," said Willie. "They're a pile of shite."

Andy held one up to the window. It had the word 'Ronda' written in red under a high, ancient-looking bridge.

"Spain," I whispered, mainly to myself.

"*Dear Julie,*" began Andy, "*the journey to Ronda was a nightmare. My mother-in-law pointed out every cow, church, dog and lamppost, like they were the most amazing things on the planet. It completely did my nut in. The running commentary only stopped when a wasp flew into the car and got caught in her blue rinse. She began screaming as it flew into the back of the car, so Ian pulled over and opened the doors while I smacked the wasp dead with a copy of the People's Friend. Said mother-in-law, rather than thank me for saving her from a nasty sting and the ensuing anaphylactic shock, refused to speak to me for the rest of the journey. It was only when we reached Ronda that Ian realised he'd driven the last ten miles with one of the back doors open. The mother-in-law's handbag was gone. Hats off to Ian, he actually sat us all in a nice café with a cool drink, before setting off back down the mountain track in search of the missing boot stock. I actually felt a pang of, what could only be described as, love."*

"How does she manage to fit all that on the one card?" asked Willie.

Andy showed us the minuscule writing that, again, strayed over into the boundary reserved for the address.

"So what are you supposed to get out of that tripe?" asked Fred.

"She said that she loved you," said Lorene.

"She never..." I began, instantly regretting it.

"She never told you that she loved you to your face?" pressed Lorene.

"Maybe she didn't want to love you," said Fred.

There was a bit of a pause before I said, "You mean, because she was just padding out a bit of time before her murdering Mafia dad and her real boyfriend got out of jail?"

"Pretty much," said Fred.

"And what about the good times we had?" I said, more than a hint of venom evident in my voice.

"What, sex?" said Andy.

"She was probably thinking about someone else," added Willie.

I swung a punch at Willie but he ducked and I caught Fred square in the jaw.

His dazzling teeth clanked together like a man trap. Blood sprayed out of his mouth and he reeled back, his eyes rolling.

As Fred slumped down his seat, I heard him choke.

"Quickly," said Lorene, "he's swallowed his tongue."

Willie yelped like a seal before helping Lorene prize Fred's jaws apart. Lorene stuck her fingers inside his mouth and hooked a tongue slick with blood out of his windpipe.

Fred spluttered and coughed before sitting bolt upright. Tears were streaming down his face as he turned to face me. "You..." he pointed a shaky finger at me.

"I didn't mean to hit you," I protested.

"If the Mafia don't get you, I fucking will!" Fred coughed.

There was a rap on the window of the van and we all jumped.

A ticket inspector stood outside busily scribbling on his clipboard. "Biglettos!"

"Shit, we need a ticket," said Andy. He rolled the passenger-side window down and Lorene leaned over to speak. She handed the guy a credit card and paid.

You could have cut the tension with a knife as we climbed out of the van. Willie rescued his bass guitar from the back of the van, and I grabbed my Les Paul.

I wasn't the kind of guitarist who practised much. I'd put the time in when I was a teenager. Ten hours a day, learning every riff and solo I could get my hands on. This put me in good stead. I hadn't really improved much since then, but that time and investment had been good enough to carry me through twenty years of gigs.

The reason I pulled my guitar out from the jumble of stands and drum cases was purely to avoid being anywhere near Fred.

Andy had led him, complaining and spouting threats, towards the lifts.

I looked behind me and saw Lorene, like a slender shadow, patiently waiting.

"Do you think we're safe here?" I asked her.

Her full lips formed a coy smile. "Smacking a Glaswegian gangster in the face hasn't helped much."

"Naw," moaned Willie. He prodded me with his case. "What the fuck ...?"

"I was aiming for you, you prick. If you hadn't ducked like a sissy, good old Uncle Fred wouldn't have got a smack in the first place."

"Enough!" hissed Lorene.

"You there!"

We all turned to see one of the crew walking purposely towards us.

Lorene reached behind her back for her gun.

"I thought you said you couldn't make it?" he said.

I gave the man in uniform a bemused look.

"You're the blues band, 'The Cryin' Shame', right?"

Willie beamed. "Yeah, that's right."

"I'm John Willman, Dolph Lines." He stretched out a hand.

I shook it briskly, then followed him into a staff elevator.

"It's a five-hour crossing to Olbia," he explained. "We have a back line and a set of drums all ready to go."

"Where's Andy?" I whispered to Willie.

"I'll call him," said Willie, already dialling.

"Is she the singer?" he asked.

Lorene shook her head. "I'm the groupie."

Willie stopped talking into his phone and smiled sardonically. "Now you're talking."

The Dolph Lines guy raised his eyebrows then turned and walked us along a narrow corridor. It seemed to run behind the main passenger areas. Eventually, he opened a heavy, black door that led straight onto a stage in the main lounge. "Ninety percent of the staff speak Italian, so call me if you need anything. You start at twelve. Three forty-five minute sets as agreed."

I nodded and began looking over the equipment. There was a 30-watt valve amp for my guitar and a bass combo for Willie. It looked as though they'd adapted an old in-house P.A. by hooking up a couple of powered speakers, and all the mics and leads required were in place. A battered drum kit was wedged in at the back of the stage.

"So, where do you think 'The Cryin' Shame' have got to?" I asked Willie.

"Who gives a fuck?" he answered.

Andy appeared with a very angry-looking Uncle Fred in tow. "I keep telling him," said Andy, "that you meant to hit Willie."

"Yeah," I said, busy adjusting the tone on my amp while hitting an A major, "I meant to..."

"Save it," snapped Fred. His lip was cut and he was missing one of his crowns. He suddenly looked less like a Glaswegian dandy and more like a street fighter. I could see the rough edges now: his mean eyes, puffy and determined, like a boxer's. And his grey, stubbly face; a mishmash of lines and scars from a thousand brawls. There was a smudge of fake tan on his ridiculous shirt collar.

"So," said Lorene, "I get to hear you play again? It's good," she continued, "I can hang back and see if anyone is acting suspiciously." She looked at Fred quizzically, then said, "You can be my sugar daddy. We'll stand over there."

Before she moved off, I signalled Lorene to come closer.

"What is it?" she whispered. "You going to put your tongue in my mouth again?"

I blinked in surprise. "Only if you want me to."

She narrowed her eyes and stared me out.

I didn't know what to do or say. "Is there …? I mean, am I missing something?"

"Play 'Bling Blang Bong'," she said, mischievously.

"How do you know about that?"

"That and much more besides," she said, "like you being the Scottish Junior Karate Champion when you were fifteen."

My stomach turned. "I gave that up. I told you why."

She nodded. "You still have the muscle memory, but I think you're getting mixed up."

"What?"

"When you blinded that boy, you had been out to get him back for all the bullying … No?" said Lorene.

"I knew I could take him if he tried it again, that's all."

"But you were still hoping he would come at you?"

"I suppose," I answered.

"That was wrong, but now it's different. You never went to 'seek out and maim' classes, you went to self-defence classes, right?"

I could see now what Lorene was getting at. I'd given up on karate because I knew I had used it wrongly. But now I was using it to protect myself, nothing more. "So, you think I should get back into it again?"

"Why not? You are older and wiser now."

I laughed. "Maybe."

She moved a little closer and, in a husky tone, said, "I may need your help, so use it if you have to."

I flushed red before changing the subject. "So," I said, "are the Savianos and Galdinis holding off?" I looked about nervously.

"We'd all be dead by now if they weren't," she said.

The passengers began to filter into the bar and as soon as

Andy settled behind his kit, we kicked off with 'Bad Moon Rising', the old Credence Clearwater Revival number. My amp had a nice crunch to it. Valve amps were living things. They had a growl and bite all of their own. Each one was different, and this one had been broken in nicely. I closed my eyes and the music took me far away from Mafia hit men, the roll of the sea, and the wife I'd never really known.

CHAPTER TWENTY-THREE

During the first set I managed to remember some material from over twelve years ago. These were songs I'd played only once or twice, in very early bands. And as I dug them out, from God knows where, I began to recall my first meeting with Maria.

Sometimes songs can act like a trigger. They can make you relive, almost re-experience things in a really vivid way: a scent, an emotion, another sound, a place, someone's face...

In my case, it was 'Pretty Woman' by Roy Orbison. As soon as I hit the opening riff I could smell the sea, feel the sun, warm as a blanket, on my face. I could hear Maria laughing, her voice still young and full of wonder. I could see her, standing on the white sand, smiling at me. She was wearing a navy-blue dress and her hair was as black as a raven's wing. I remembered wandering over to speak to her. It took every ounce of courage I could muster at the time. We walked and talked for hours and, later, as we sat above the beach amongst the wild flowers, we held hands. It wasn't a sham. My life... our love... the good times, none of it. It couldn't have been.

Willie squinted over at me as I blanked on the verse. He held up three fingers, which was our code for 'wanker', and took over the lead vocal.

Free from the confines of my microphone stand, I was able to pick out Lorene in the audience. Fred was standing at the bar with another woman. It was dark and the stage lights were shining right into my eyes, but my heart sank.

I spun round to face Andy, the band time-keeper, and in an urgent voice yelled, "Have we done forty-five minutes yet?"

Andy gave me the thumbs up and then we all finished the song: "Yeah... Yeah... Pretty woman!"

The house lights came on and I slipped the strap of the heavy Les Paul over my head. I caught Willie before he left the stage. "Did you see the woman who was standing beside Lorene? She had short dark hair"

He waved me away. "What woman? I'm going to get wrecked."

"Oh, great idea," I shouted after him. "We've got half of Italy after us and you want to get pissed."

He only gave me two fingers this time.

I put my Gibson back in its case, the safest place for a two-thousand-quid guitar when there's no guitar stand, and began picking my way through the audience.

Lorene was still at the bar but she was alone.

"Where's Fred?" I asked.

"He can't go far," she remarked, "unless he can swim a hundred miles of Tyrrhenian Sea, he's going to be on this boat when we need him."

"I … I thought I saw you both talking to a woman," I said.

Lorene shrugged. "I don't think you saw right."

"She had short, dark hair. She was about so high." I held my hand about three inches above Lorene's head.

"I am more concerned about those guys across there," said Lorene.

I could see Willie being accosted by a group of men who looked as if they were complimenting him on his bass-playing. Now this was normal for lead guitar playing, singing or even drumming–but punters getting excited about bass playing? It just didn't happen.

"Where's he going?" I said. "We're back on stage in twenty minutes."

Willie was chatting to the girl with the short dark hair. Not his type. Far too young and petite. And now he was following her outside onto the deck. "Willie!" I turned to Lorene. "What's he doing?"

It was around 7pm, and there was a strong wind outside, so most of the passengers had elected to remain inside.

"We better go see what he's is up to," said Lorene.

"You might get more than you bargained for," I muttered.

Keeping out of sight, we followed Willie and his new escort out onto the deck. The sun was low and it was far from warm. I had to pull my collar up against the cold.

Outside, it was pretty obvious to me that Willie had already made his move. Alone with the girl, just below the ship's tall, pale-blue funnel, Willie had put one arm around her back while the other made tentative, exploratory forays. Amazingly, she didn't seem to flinch.

I thought about this for a moment and realised that Willie must have been as rancid as Andy and me. We hadn't washed properly or changed our clothes for days.

After a quick glance round the deck to make sure no one was about, the girl, in an heroic gesture, given the weather, crouched down. She unzipped Willie's jeans and got to work.

"She's a pro," whispered Lorene. She looked behind her and began scanning the rest of the deck. "We've been set up."

"What do you mean?" I asked, trying my best to keep up with her.

"We need to find Fred," she said.

I shouted after her. "I told you this was dodgy."

We raced past a deserted sunbathing deck and made for the front of the ship, but there was no one there. Just a bored-looking deckhand coating a door with varnish.

"Shit! What is wrong with me," shouted Lorene. She drew her gun and began jogging back to the stern.

I looked at my mobile. "We're due back on stage in ten minutes," I reminded.

"If you are going to throw someone off a moving ship, it is always better to do it at the stern!" she shouted over her shoulder.

I was wheezing like mad by the time we'd reached the giant blue chimney again. Willie and the girl were gone.

Lorene tore down a set of stairs and I followed.

Halfway down, it was obvious that she'd been right. Gathered round the back rail of the ship, I could see a group of men, the same men we'd seen in the bar chatting to Willie. They were holding someone against the white railing.

I immediately recognised his tanned, bald head. "They've got Fred," I gasped.

Two men had pinned Fred's arms tight to the rails, like he was on a cross, while a third pointed straight at his face.

Lorene knelt and steadied her aim. "We have to get closer." She scampered down the metal staircase, the wind masking her footsteps.

Cold and shaking with terror, I followed Lorene as she lighted on the deck and walked boldly towards the group of men. "Don't move!"

Two of the men drew their own guns and pointed them straight back at us.

I wondered why Lorene hadn't fired sooner.

The man who'd been pointing at Fred's face turned slowly, and forced a smile. It was Carlos Azuni. "This is none of your business, Miss Duval."

"Let him go!" I yelled, somewhat pathetically.

A cold voice called from above, "Drop your weapon."

I stared up at the girl who'd been with Willie. She had something that looked like an Uzi, pointing straight at us.

Lorene placed her gun down on the deck. "Sorry, Ian, I think I've let you down this time."

I could see the Italians beginning to smile as their bravado returned.

Without looking at Fred, Carlos took a machete from the inside of his jacket and said, "Hold his arm straight."

"No!" barked Fred, "I have the key. You can have the case." His wrist was exposed. A metal cuff supported a chain which in turn suspended the swaying attaché case.

"No!" Yelled Willie. "Leave him alone."

"Well," said Carlos, "that changes everything."

Fred smiled, but only for a second before Carlos brought his machete down in a neat arc.

There was an ear-splitting scream and the attaché case, plus Fred's hand and wrist, dropped to the deck.

"Get the key off of him," he said to one of his men.

Blood spouted out of Fred's wrist. He was losing consciousness.

Willie was going crazy, but one of the heavies has his gun pointing right at his face. "You fucking bastards. You fucking–"

"Pull him up," said Carlos. He moved within a few inches of Fred's face. "You don't come into my place and rob me. You don't side with a Galdini against me and my business."

"Please... I won't do it..."

"Again?" said Carlos, a sardonic smile forming on his face. "There will be no second chance for you, Mr Marvin." With that, he caught a swaying Fred by the balls and his bloody arm, heaved him up and then over the back of the ship.

"No!" Willie was in tears.

Fred disappeared amongst the foam and the dark water. He never even bobbed back up again. He just vanished.

Like a bunch of tourists, we all clutched onto the back rail.

I was almost sick on the spot.

"Bastard!" spat Lorene. "There was no need to do that."

"There was every need," said Carlos, "you know the rules, Miss Duval–an eye for an eye..." He turned to face Willie. "Now what shall I do with you?"

"Carlos. He knew nothing about the money," I yelled.

Carlos tilted his head as if examining his prey before the final bite. "No... I don't think he did." He moved back. "What about you, Miss Duval?"

I moved forward and, as the heavy next to Willie turned his aim on me, I lunged sideways and knocked the gun from his hand. "Leave her alone!" I was holding the gun to Carlos' throat, shaking like mad.

Carlos squinted down at me. "Impressive. Has Miss Duval been giving you lessons?"

The girl with the short hair was right beside me, the Uzi pointed at my face.

"Lower your aim, Sasha," said Carlos.

Sasha did as she was instructed.

"Leave it, Ian," said Lorene. "Drop the gun."

Carlos stared at Lorene a little longer. "Are you mixing business with pleasure, Miss Duval? How very unprofessional."

I let the gun fall. We were all still in shock.

"Now, go and finish your little gig. Get off this boat and remain in the town of Obila. Once I'm sure, I will tell you exactly where to meet Maria."

Sasha and the henchmen seemed to disappear into the shadows and Carlos was about to leave too, when I asked, "What about the Galdinis? Are they still after us?"

"Antonio Galdini is a madman," whispered Carlos. "For centuries, we've been able to pick and choose which side we worked for, but now..."

"Now that my wife is set to marry Franco Galdini," I interrupted, "you will end up working for your enemy?"

"In a manner of speaking," said Carlos, "and that would have been fine until today." He slipped a very old-looking letter from his long coat and opened it. "This," he whispered, "came into my possession today."

I waited, confused and still very anxious.

"It is from another member of the Azuni family." Carlos stared straight at me. "A man you met twenty years ago."

I couldn't think. "What, at our wedding?"

Carlos grunted. "Huh. That was no more than playacting. No. You met this man on a beach. You probably don't remember, but he—"

"—he waded out into the sea with Maria and pulled a dead dog out of the water?" I finished.

Carlos nodded. "Exactly. That was my father. He died that day."

"I'm sorry. We called that place 'Dead Dog Beach' after that," I said, my head still spinning. "And he gave Maria a key... it was attached to the dead dog's collar."

"That key was never attached the dog's collar," said Carlos. "My father was brilliant at improvisation. He came to that beach to make sure Maria made the pact with you, but he was frail. He gave her the key, not to remind her of her promise to her father and the Galdinis, but as insurance. The key was the Azunis' 'get out of jail card'."

"I don't understand," said Lorene, "what significance does a letter from your father have now?"

"How did you get it?" I added.

"The letter? It was found it in the ruins of my father's house. It said that he was going to give a special key to Maria."

"Well, he did that, and I'm guessing you knew it was a key to a locker in the Redante," I surmised.

"The locker was empty," said Carlos. "I checked it years ago. I'm afraid the secret of the 'four judges' burial site died with my father."

I could see Willie was still staring out over the sea. "Otherwise, you could have revealed the site to the authorities and both families would have gone down."

"Everyone apart from the Azunis," said Lorene. "You would be perfectly placed to take over both families' interests. What else did the letter say?"

Carlos gave Lorene a sideways look. "The letter also said that key would reveal the site of the 'four judges' burial ground."

"But it didn't," said Lorene.

"My father was ninety. Maybe he never got a chance to put the coordinates in the locker," said Carlos. "You are our only hope, Mr Angus."

Willie seemed to shake himself back to realty. "Why the fuck are you even talking to this monster?" He stabbed an accusing finger at Carlos.

"Your uncle was using you," said Carlos.

I glanced down at the pool of blood, the briefcase, the chain, and the severed hand.

Carlos threw the hand overboard and picked up the case. "I usually kill kin like you, Willie. Relatives that might one day come back for revenge, but I need him." Carlos pointed to me. "So, for now, he's saved your life." He turned and went through a door marked private.

Willie, Lorene and myself were standing by ourselves as the sun edged down below the horizon.

Willie turned on me. He grabbed my collar and pinned me to the rail. "My uncle came here to help you. To help us..."

Lorene, in turn, caught Willie by the shoulder. Not aggressively, but gently, and said, "He came here to help himself, Willie. I am not condoning what Carlos did, but he was right about your uncle."

CHAPTER TWENTY-FOUR

To my surprise, and indeed horror, someone else was playing my guitar when we found Andy inside at the bar.

"That Italian guy playing your guitar is a pure genius. Did you hear him?" said Andy enthusiastically.

"Why the hell is he playing my guitar?"

"No, really, he makes that old guitar of yours actually sing," he continued. "He's kept this place spellbound for about half an hour. Just him and the guitar."

"Thanks, Andy," I said. "Why don't you just say that I'm shit and he's great. Don't beat about the bush."

"There are more important things," Lorene interrupted.

"What?" said Andy, now distracted by Willie, who was edging, clumsily, towards us. "Has he been drinking?" Andy looked about the bar. "Where's Fred?"

Willie stopped dead, in front of Andy. "They killed Uncle Fred."

Andy's mouth fell open. "Who killed…Uncle Fred's dead?"

"He had stolen money from the Azunis," said Lorene.

"The briefcase?" muttered Andy.

I nodded. "They... Carlos Azuni threw him overboard."

"What? He's dead?"

"They cut his fuckin' hand off and threw him into the sea. He never came back up," said Willie.

Lorene grabbed Willie's hand and led him from the bar.

"Where is she taking him?" hissed Andy.

I shrugged. "He's totally screwed up. It all happened pretty quickly."

"The removal guy?" said Andy.

"Yes. Carlos Azuni," I said. "He knows where Maria is and he wants me to persuade her to come back home with us."

"And you're going to do him a favour after he killed Fred?" pressed Andy.

"Andy," I said, "why are we fuckin' here?"

Andy looked bemused. He was probably trying to take it all in.

"We are here so I can get to Maria and persuade her to come home."

Andy walked across to the guy who was still playing my guitar and switched off the amp. "Sorry. We're finishing up."

"Okay." The guy stood up and got a round of applause.

Andy must have clocked me looking at Lorene at the bar with Willie. "But you like her now, don't you?"

"That's not the point."

"It kinda is," said Andy. "The postcards, everything Maria is mixed up in, if I were you I would…"

"Well, you're not me, so shut it," I blurted.

Andy looked pale. "I'm not sure I can do this anymore."

"You're doing it. We are all doing it, okay?"

Andy gave a reluctant nod.

* * *

Willie still looked like death warmed up as I drove our new white van out of the bowels of the ferry. I accelerated up the metal tongue of the ship in a dark mood. Braking harshly, I turned left onto a shore road that skirted a couple of high buildings before leaving the port behind. "Welcome to the Costa Esmeralda," I said.

"I can't believe he's dead," moaned Willie. "What am I going to tell Aunt Jessie?"

"Those who live by the sword usually die by it," said Lorene, cheerfully.

"You live by the sword," said Andy, turning round in his seat to look at Lorene.

"And I expect to die by it too," she replied. "It's all part of the deal."

"You don't expect to be thrown off a moving ferry, twenty miles from shore, then left to drown alone," said Willie.

"Those rails were a good sixty feet above the water, Willie," explained Andy, "he was probably knocked out or killed by the fall."

Willie spun round in his seat to look at Andy who was sitting next to Lorene on the bench behind us. "Will you shut the fuck up. I don't care what anyone says, Uncle Fred came out here to help us."

"We've been over this," interrupted Lorene. "He met with Galdini first, remember."

Willie was about to fire one back but instead, he eased back into the front seat and stared gloomily into the middle distance.

"There's only a few of those cards left to read, Ian, if you want to take your mind off things a bit," suggested Andy.

"Fuck off with those postcards," snapped Willie.

"No," said Lorene, "there might be a clue in them that can help us."

Willie sighed and punched the inside of the passenger door.

"There's only two left," said Andy, waving a postcard at me in the rear-view mirror. He ducked down again and began searching inside his bag. "Hey, where's my mobile?"

"Why?" I asked.

"I've arranged gigs and stuff."

"Carlos said to wait until he phoned me," I explained.

"Why should we do what he says?" said Andy.

I tensed. "When it comes right down to it, you don't really give a shit, do you Andy?"

"I give a shit but–"

"No you don't," I snapped. "This is just a few more gigs to you, isn't it? An adventure."

"It's a fuckin' frightening one," said Andy. "I just don't get whose side we're on. Azuni warns us off at your place then he captures you and Lorene at the casino, then he lets you go, then his men try to shoot Fred, then he turns up in person and kills him. Then he tells you he needs your help to stop two big Mafia families intermarrying because it's going to put his family out of a job."

"Shut up and read us a fuckin' card," said Willie, in a loud, pissed-off voice.

Andy exhaled and produced a trail of swear words before pinging a card free and saying, "This one..." He turned the card over in his hands, "is from La Rochelle."

"Jesus," I moaned.

Andy sneered. "It says: *'Dear Julie, It's been in the high thirties and I made Ian take me and the his nephews to the beach. A two-hour drive and another hour trying to find a parking space was beginning to test his patience. Despite this, however, kids in tow, he dragged two prams, a heavy bag and a parasol over 300 yards of blistering hot sand until we found a four-foot patch of sand covered in fag ends. We sat tight for a moment, but then the kids began scrapping. I nagged and nagged Ian to sort it out and he eventually snapped. He was actually aiming to give the oldest, Ryan, a brisk smack on the back of the legs but Ryan dropped to his knees and turned at the wrong moment and got a slap in the mouth instead. His braces spiralled out of his mouth in a trail of blood, like some slow-motion Kung Fu film, and he began howling like a banshee. The French sunbathers all scowling at us, began tapping on their mobile phones, as though they were all calling Childline en masse. So, we packed up and left without so much as a petit baguette or a paddle in the waves. I find it hard to blame Ian this time. What's wrong with me? Heatstroke?*

Maria.'

"And the point of this tale is?" asked Willie through a yawn.

"The point," began Lorene, "is that Maria didn't have 'heatstroke'. She was in love. She may have started out by pretending to be the happy wife, but she grew to love Ian. She is trying to tell you that, no matter what; she fell in love with you. It may have been years after you thought she had, but main point is that she did."

"We never had kids" I mused.

"No fuckin' wonder," said Andy, "She knew you were going to smack them in the mouth one day."

"Sounds like the little shit deserved it," said Lorene.

"It was a really stressful day," I added. "I felt terrible when I saw the blood..."

"Was it a Kung Fu punch?" said Willie.

This was the first glimmer of the Willie we all knew since he saw his uncle launched over the side of a boat.

Lorene's mobile rang. She cupped it, listened and then said, "Where? When?"

I pulled the van over to the side of the road.

"It was Carlos Azuni," she said, folding her mobile away. "He wants Ian and Willie to meet him at the back of the Hotel Rene Cagliari, beside the bins, at the electric gate."

"When?" I said.

"After you've played you've played your first set."

"Shit," I muttered. I was really scared. "The resort is three hours away yet."

"Why do I have to be there?" whispered Willie. "I don't have to be there."

"You better do as he says," Lorene said.

"Look, it's only five. We'll make it to Cagliari no bother," said Andy, ignoring Willie, "and that entertainment guy on the boat gave me this." He held up a brown envelope. "Two hundred euros."

"Did you tell him we weren't his band?" I asked.

"Yeah, but he still paid up. Said that guitarist was the best he'd ever heard. Said the punters loved it. Loads of them said it was the best ferry trip they'd ever had."

"Fuck off, Andy," I mumbled.

"For some, it was the last ferry trip they ever had," muttered Willie.

Andy bit down on a smile and then, trying his best to look concerned, said, "He was an evil fuck anyway."

"How do you know?" said Willie.

"You told me," said Andy, "plenty of times."

I nodded. "And so did the papers."

"They never had anything on him," said Willie.

"Well, he might have been careful in Glasgow but he slipped up here."

"Now we're in Sardinia," said Lorene, "I have a feeling things could really hot up. Don't trust anyone."

"Does that include you?" asked Willie.

"It does, if you keep looking at my tits in that mirror," she rebuffed.

Willie shook his head in disbelief. "Never miss a trick, do you?"

"You'll be missing a pair of balls if you don't stop gawping," she snapped.

"Okay, okay," I said. "Let's all calm down."

"Get some sleep, Willie," barked Lorene. "I want to hear the last postcard."

"No way. They are pointless," moaned Willie.

"It's from Javea, Spain," said Andy, pinging the elastic off for the last time.

"Read it," said Lorene. She stroked my arm with her long fingers as I pulled out of the lay-by.

Andy turned it over and grimaced. "There's hardly anything written on this one–but..."

CHAPTER TWENTY-FIVE

I didn't want Andy to read anything else from Maria. I accelerated and hoped the roar of the engine would cover his inevitable sarcastic comments.

"Well?" demanded Willie. "We've travelled thousands of miles to get to this bloody island, what's the last message?"

I stared in anticipation at Andy in the mirror. He was stretching out the moment on purpose. "It says:

Dear Julie, I realise that whatever I write on this card is just going to be trivial crap compared to what's going on with you. You have a good man. You found the love of your life. I'm sure he will always be there for you. I only ever had one, as you know. I told you about Carlos once, but it was never to be."

Love you always

Maria.

There was an eerie silence for a moment before I said, "You should have read that one first."

"Yeah. It might have saved us all a lot of hassle," said Andy.

"To say the fuckin' least," added Willie.

"Julie was badly injured in a car crash," I mumbled. "She had complications and..." I couldn't take it in. The bit about Carlos. I just wanted everything to roll on the way it was playing out.

Lorene took the card from Andy's fingers and re-read it. "It must be the same Carlos, don't you think?"

"Well, we're here now so, we may as well keep to the plan."

"Keep to the plan?" said Willie. "What fuckin' plan is that?"

Andy shrugged. "To get him his wife back."

"Well, it's pretty fuckin' obvious, she never loved him and–"

"Shut up!" I shouted. I pulled the van over and stared blankly into an angry Sardinian sky. "Will you all give me a moment to get my head around this?"

"Maria obviously told her friend, Julie, about Carlos a long time ago. The card dates from four years ago," said Lorene.

I could feel the weight of their pity, anger and frustration but I knew something for sure. "I have to see her now. More than ever."

Willie grunted. "What? So, you can give her a good slap?"

Lorene bowed her head and sighed even deeper than before. "I feel sorry for her. Her life with you and the friends she made—it wasn't all a lie. Forced to marry a random Scotsman after only three weeks to keep her father safe and now, forced to marry Franco Galdini to keep the peace."

I eased my foot off the accelerator as a feeling of soul-crushing sadness flooded over me. *She'd been trapped in a kind of limbo—waiting, trying her best to keep sane by doing normal stuff, but all the time she really loved someone else.*

Willie was snoring. His six pints of lager on the ship and the shock of losing his Uncle Fred had taken their toll.

"I don't get it," said Andy. "How could she have lived a lie for so long?"

"You don't understand the power of 'the family', Andy," said Lorene. "On Sardinia or on Sicily, if you are part of 'the family', you are born into great privilege but also into great responsibility. It's even stronger than religion. Maria's sacrifice kept a war at bay for ten years and now there is chance for her to make the 'peace' between the two clans permanent."

"So why did she marry Ian after just three weeks?" asked Andy.

"She was told to," said Lorene. "I'm more interested in why Ian married her."

This was a tough one to explain. "I... She said that she was a fan. Her whole family, all of her friends, they all knew me from that one hit song. I was on TV in Europe all the time. It got played over and over..."

"So how come you've got no money? You lying bastard!" Willie snapped, suddenly awake and totally in the conversation.

"I got bugger all! I signed a stupid deal," I explained.

"Let me guess," said Andy, "We will make you famous with this song, you'll get paid for the next one?"

I looked at him for a long awkward moment. "Yeah."

"The record company fed on your self-obsession," added Lorene.

"And Maria's family..." said Andy.

"They fed on his self-obsession too," said Lorene.

I flushed red. I knew they were right. "I thought she was beautiful."

"She still is," said Lorene. She smiled to herself. "And I can see why she was attracted to you. If I had to go away for ten years to another country, with a stranger, it might as well be a good-looking one..."

I felt my face flush again. "What are you saying?"

"Yeah," added Andy, "what are you saying, Lorene?"

"Nothing like that," she snapped, drawing her hand away from my arm. "I'm thinking more of the practicalities."

"I see," said Andy, "you mean like sex and stuff."

Lorene lifted something from her bag and said, "We have an escort."

Ahead, a black sedan had slowed at a corner. I looked into the wing mirror and saw another, almost identical car, behind us. It was signalling the same way.

In a sharp whisper, Andy asked, "What should we do?"

"Nothing," said Lorene. "They're probably making sure we're on our way to the hotel, as planned. It just means that your meeting with Carlos tonight is going to need a distraction before it can happen."

"Are they Savianos or Galdinis?" asked Andy.

Lorene shrugged. "It doesn't really matter. They both want the same thing."

"Which is?" I asked.

"You 'out of the way' as soon as the wedding is over, I would suspect. They are only tolerating your presence here because of Maria. Now you've made it this far, they don't want to jeopardize the big day by killing you on home turf."

Around nine-thirty, we pulled up to a ubiquitous white building with the words–'Hotel Rene Cagliari' painted in black above the reception area. A small man in a white linen uniform guided us round the side and buzzed us through an electric gate into the car park.

It was beginning to feel humid, and I could smell that smell you get in hot countries. A kind of sweet, pungent, odour that hits you like a warm soup when you step off the plane. A smell that we, in the northern climes, find both slightly stifling, yet enticing. It signals cocktails, sunburn and freedom. It gives us permission to be excited in an alien land.

But for me, the signals were all mixed up. It now seemed like a really bad idea coming here at all. It sounded as if I'd be killed the instant Maria said, 'I do'. Whereas if I'd remained in Glasgow, I may have got away with a fairly innocuous life, albeit pathetic and unresolved.

Once inside the hotel, we went into automatic 'set up' mode. Drums first, then back-line, then the P.A. The customary 'one, two...one, two', was delivered, along with an ear-splitting stab of feedback and then we were all set. We'd never done big sound-checks in the past. They cut into our drinking time and became obsolete, an unnecessary hindrance. Instead, in the places we actually gave a shit about, the band always began with the perfect sound-check song: 'Ballroom Blitz' by Sweet. Drums first, a wee vocal check, in the 'Are you ready Steve' bit, followed by the killer guitar riff, which I extended, and finally the bass. All done. Sorted. And off we went.

On this occasion the holiday reps had organised a hula hoop competition, which was pretty good, because everyone made a right arse of themselves, except a forty-something stunner who gyrated and wiggled her way to the first prize, every part of her moving in perfect unison. Then we were on. Pints were positioned and the lights came on as we kicked off with 'Sweet Home Alabama'.

Inevitably, a few tables, only inches from the stage, began to empty, and we were told to turn it down.

It's practically impossible to play rock quietly. The thing about volume is that you have to reach critical mass—a level where you feel part of your instrument. The valves need to cook and the speakers should be at full tilt—otherwise, you can't 'get into it'. And if you can't get enthused, lost in the music, then there's no fucking chance that the audience will either.

All this pent-up frustration kept me from being quite as terrified as I should have been.

First set completed, we grabbed a table and sat down.

"No one's dancing," moaned Willie. "Bunch of fuckers."

"Yeah, let's turn it up, do some Lizzy," added Andy.

Lorene sipped her lemonade and glanced at me inquisitively.

"And how many times have we played a gig where no one dances in the first set?" I said.

They both sighed and shrugged.

"Every fucking gig is the same, and you still get all paranoid. People need to trust you, be pissed enough to dance and stuff..." I tapped my temple with my forefinger. "We know this to be true."

"So?" muttered Willie. "They're still a bunch of fuckers."

A woman who reeked of fags and sweat suddenly stopped at our table and leaned into me. "Do you know any Pink Floyd?" she asked in a Newcastle accent.

"No, sorry," I said.

I stared in desperation at Willie and Andy. She'd just sprayed my ear with spittle.

"What about Rush?" she asked, dousing me even more.

Lorene was actually giggling.

The woman then plumped herself on my knee and began trying to stick her vodka-flavoured tongue down my throat.

"Look! No... I don't," I protested.

Willie and Andy were gutting themselves.

"Why do you always get them?" said Andy.

When I tried to remove her from my knee, she stood up and slapped me.

"Useless fucker!" she shouted at me, before addressing a mainly disinterested audience, "They can't even play Rush!" I received a final one-finger salute and then she was gone.

Lorene's eyes were wide with amazement.

"No, it's normal," explained Andy, through a cascade of tears. "He always gets the bunny boilers."

"Speaking of which," said Willie, his voice full of foreboding.

CHAPTER TWENTY-SIX

I followed Willie's gaze and eventually picked out the girl with the short dark hair that had accosted Willie on the ferry.

"Carlos must be here already," said Lorene.

The girl was walking straight towards us, a look of grim determination on her face

Willie got up from his chair, his mood suddenly dark, his eyes wild. "She was in on the whole thing. I'll kill her."

"Whoa there, Bald Eagle," I advised, "she won't be alone."

"It's time we went backstage," said Lorene. She caught Willie's arm and pulled him out of his seat.

We all got up and followed her, as if we were simply going to go back on for the second set. But, once on stage, we edged through the velvet curtain and scrambled over a mishmash of old lighting rigs towards the fire escape.

A holiday rep had followed us. He called out, "What about your second set?"

"Do another hula hoop competition," replied Andy. "We won't be long."

Lorene pushed down on the bar of the fire escape and it swung out into the night air. A solitary green light shone down from above the door, stretching our shadows out along the tarmac outside. All four of us braced, half-expecting a burst of gunfire or at least a shout of warning. But there was nothing. Just the hum of the electrics and the rattle of cicadas.

"Now what?" whispered Andy.

"We wait by the bins around the corner, as Carlo instructed," said Lorene.

We could hear people moving across the metal stanchions at the back of the stage.

"Follow me," said Lorene, drawing her gun.

"Shit," hissed Willie, "why did I ever agree to come on this fucked up tour?"

I heard the thump of a bullet in a tree ahead of us.

"This way!" snapped Lorene.

I followed her, hoping Willie and Andy were keeping up. Almost in complete darkness, I raced down an embankment and veered left. I could hear the sea, lapping against the shore. My legs shuddered as I hit the sand.

We skirted the promenade, keeping as tight as we could to a wall on our left as we ran. We dodged bins and one startled couple before crouching down behind a neat pile of chained-up sun beds.

There were no more bullets, only the sound of our own laboured breathing.

"There," whispered Andy, "at the other end of the beach."

I screwed up my eyes and watched a group of men fan out over the sand about three hundred metres away. Now we had pursuers behind us and in front.

"None of these people are Azuni's men," whispered Lorene. "I think you've just become fair game, Ian."

"Brilliant," I whispered back, suddenly wondering if I'd die here on this Sardinian beach before I'd even had the chance to see Maria again.

Lorene pulled up the leg of her jeans and unravelled something. I saw her screw it onto her gun.

"It's a silencer," whispered Willie.

"When I bring the first two down, the rest of those guys coming towards us will take cover. So, when I fire, you run for those trees, ahead and to the left."

I could just make out some tall shadows a hundred yards further on, under a street light.

Andy caught my sleeve. "There must be another way to–"

A couple of thuds echoed across the beach in rapid succession and two of group coming towards us dropped like stones. One clutched his chest, the other his throat.

I felt Willie's hand heave me forwards and I was running again, at full pelt.

I heard another thud of a bullet behind me but I didn't look back, I just kept on moving as fast as I could.

We dived into the trees and wedged ourselves behind a low, crumbling wall.

"Is Lorene hit?" I panted.

"I don't think so," said Willie. He issued a series of stifled coughs.

Undeterred, the cicadas continued to fill the warm air with their din. One of them sounded as if it was in my hair, it was so fucking loud.

Voices sounded to our right. There were other people in the woods with us. Everyone must have made for the same spot.

"Shit!" hissed Andy.

A man's shadow crept right over our position, but we all remained as still as we could. It was only when he literally stood on Willie's hand that our bass player acted.

He brought his free hand up in a fist and slammed it into the guy's groin.

The guy exhaled but before he could scream out, Willie caught his collar and pulled him down hard onto the wall. I heard him bite down on his own tongue. Although I could do a few moves, I could never match Willie's sheer level of violence.

Andy and myself pinned the guy to the ground while Willie pounded his head and face with his fists. One of Willie's punches caught him on the temple and the man stopped moving.

All around us, more people were edging through the undergrowth.

I held my breath and waited.

Five seconds later, all hell broke out.

Machine guns rattled out over the beach in all directions and a hail of bullets ripped the branches above us to shreds. Leaves and twigs rained down on our heads as men ran past us and began shouting commands to each other.

I could hear someone screaming about twenty metres away.

I nudged Andy. "We need to keep going." I got to my knees. A twig snapped beside me and then I felt a kick to my ribs.

"Don't move, you little–"

But my attacker never finished his sentence.

There was a muffled struggle and then the sound of a knife slicing through gristle and bone.

Warm liquid was pouring all over my face. I spat and rolled away from two people grappling above me. There was another cutting sound and then a thump as a body hit the ground.

"Follow me," whispered Lorene.

We all got up and dashed after her. Running blindly, hoping that the heavies on the beach, and the people who'd stepped over us, would continue shooting at each other. The flicking sound of leaves torn to shreds by bullets eventually died away and we staggered out into a clearing.

Lorene signalled us to stop.

Ahead of us, next to a jeep with the engine still running, was the girl with the short hair we'd seen on the ferry.

Lorene raised her gun and the girl raised her hands.

"If you want to live, you better get in," she said. Her accent sounded Russian.

"Sasha?" I asked.

"Right," she answered.

"Why should we trust you?" said Willie.

The girl gave him a sideways glance. "If I'd wanted to kill you, I could have killed you on the boat." She ignored Lorene and jumped into the driving seat. "I'm leaving with or without you."

Lorene nodded and we all jumped in.

The jeep skidded back for a few yards and then spun round, a hundred and eighty degrees, before bumping onto a tarmac road.

"You work for Carlos," said Lorene.

"You know I do," answered the girl. "He sent me to tell you that he would have to reschedule meeting. They have moved Maria Saviano further into mountains. Called off amnesty on you."

"They want to kill Ian?" panted Andy.

"Both families have contracts on all of you," she said. "Antonio Galdini and Charles Saviano have decided to remove any threat to wedding."

"So, where are you taking us?" asked Lorene.

"To Maria Saviano's new location," said the girl. "If we make it, you will have an hour to change her mind about big wedding day." She stared at me in the mirror and I saw the glint of a smile in the moonlight. "If we make it," she repeated.

CHAPTER TWENTY-SEVEN

We soon veered off the main road and began to climb up a dirt track. Sasha was driving like a maniac but none of us said anything. Even Lorene was holding on for dear life as we bounced and juddered up the mountainside.

"I only hope there has not been more subsidence since last time I vos here," said the girl in her stilted accent.

In the full beams of the jeep I could see where the track had literally fallen off the side of the mountain. Long tracts of scree and rubble marked the damage but, equally, there seemed to have been repairs carried out.

"Hold on," she yelled, "I kill lights."

"Why the fuck would anyone turn the headlights off on this excuse for a road?" moaned Andy, just before everything went pitch black.

The jeep powered on, turning sharply and dipping down small inclines.

"She's gonna kill us all!" screamed Andy.

Lorene slapped him on the back of the head and pointed to the girl's face.

As my eyes began to adjust, I could see that she was now wearing goggles.

"Infrared," explained Lorene. "Russian issue?"

The girl seemed to nod as we banged down hard into a pothole. "They vill soon realise you have escaped and call in more help," said the girl.

"What kind of help?" whined Andy.

"Helicopters, dogs ... more backup," said the girl, cheerfully.

"For the love of fuck," cried Andy.

"They better not touch my Fender Precision," said Willie.

"Shite," I whispered, "my Les Paul isn't even in its case."

Willie looked at me and gasped, "Fuck! You're soaking wet." He shuffled away from me.

"It's only blood," said Lorene.

I trailed my fingers through the tugs in my hair.

"Look on the bright side," Lorene continued, "it's not your blood."

I shivered as we gained altitude, wondering what I would say to Maria, if we ever made it that far.

The road evened off a little and, as the moon brightened, our driver began to talk, "The clans thought you would be safe, down in Cagliari. Far enough away from Maria, in the north, to do any harm; but when they found out about Fred Marvin…"

"How did they find out?" I asked.

I thought I saw the girl shrug. "Who knows?"

"They probably had a passenger list," said Andy.

"Jesus," muttered Willie, "why did you have to kill him?"

"That is the point," said the girl. "There is rumour that *you* threw him overboard."

"Me?" yelped Willie.

"Big rumour. Not just you. All of you," she said. "Suddenly, you not so harmless." She laughed to herself and brought the jeep to a halt at a crossroads.

"Are you saying that the police are after us?" I asked.

"Don't be stupid," she said, "they are always last to know anything."

"But it's all lies," said Willie.

"It doesn't matter about truth," said the girl, "you are here, with me, running for lives."

"How far until we get to Maria?" I asked.

The girl swung east and we began to descend for the first time in a while. "It is still not confirmed you meet her."

"I thought you said I would have an hour to talk to her?"

But the girl didn't answer me. We just drove for miles, slowly creeping down towards sea-level again. After an hour or so, she took a sharp left and parked up in an olive grove. I could hear waves crashing in the distance, barely audible over the constant rattle and hum of the insects.

Lorene helped the girl pull some bags from the back of the jeep and we all helped to put up two canvas tents. They both stunk of wet dog and were peppered with holes.

"Where did you get these shit tents?" said Willie.

"The fuckin' tea bag factory, if you ask me" said Andy.

"It will not rain tonight," said the girl, staring up at the star-filled sky. She pointed to one of the tents. "Bed."

Willie smiled. "If you insist."

The girl waved his suggestion away. "Fuck off, smelly man. My boss has not said dis time."

We all laughed, even Lorene.

Willie grumbled a few choice words and disappeared into the tent.

"Sasha, isn't it?" I said.

"Yes," she said, smiling. "You don't smell so bad as the ginger one, but you need wash blood off. Here, take." She threw me a bar of soap and a towel, then pointed to a water container in the back of the jeep. "There are clothes in there too. Change for wife."

I asked Andy if he wanted a wash too, but he just yawned and followed Willie into his tent.

On my return, Lorene caught my arm and led me into the other tent. "He stays with me."

Before we ducked inside, Sasha revealed a set of extra-white teeth. She had a slightly fuller figure than Lorene, and looked a little younger.

"What's a Russian girl doing working for the Azuni family in Sardinia?" I asked.

"At least *she* knows who she is working for," said Lorene.

"But I thought you preferred it that way?" I said.

"I thought I did." Lorene loosened her belt and threw a sleeping bag onto the groundsheet. "You sleep there."

"And you?" I asked.

She took off her clothes and stood naked in the shadows of the tent. "Are you sure you want your wife back?"

I knelt on top of the sleeping bag, as if I was kneeling at the feet of some mythological deity. "Why wouldn't I? Just because she has a Mafia family, duped me for ten years, has a love of her life that isn't me, and is about to marry another man, doesn't mean she's all bad."

Lorene smiled and eased herself into her own sleeping bag. "We should both sleep. We can't hide on this island forever."

I could hear Andy and Willie talking in the other tent.

"We still have two days before Maria gets married again," I

said.

"Oh, I doubt that very much," whispered Lorene.

"What do you mean?"

"Sasha has already told me that the wedding has been moved forward. You will only have that one hour she promised you."

"So, I might see her once tomorrow and then..."

"Then..." said Lorene, sitting up, "then you will either persuade her to come back with you or she will head off and get married a few hours later."

"A few hours?"

Lorene shrugged and lay back. "What have you learned about yourself this week, Ian?"

"Me?"

"It's always all about you..." Lorene laughed.

"I guess you have a point. I was a bit 'me, me, me...'"

"A bit?"

"And you have other skills, apart from playing guitar." Lorene sat up again.

"What? You mean like kissing?" I could see Lorene's white teeth in the gloom of the tent.

"Maybe. I forget?"

"You forget?" I moved a little closer.

"I've been a self-centred asshole for most of my life. Is that what you want to hear?"

"Keep going. It's turning me on."

I moved even closer. "I've let my vanity and pride, lust for fame and fortune cloud everything I've ever done."

"And?" Lorene crawled towards me like a leopard.

"And I don't want to forget this...ever."

Lorene wrapped her arms around me and I felt her lithe, smooth body against mine. My head was saying that this was wrong, especially after all I'd been through to get this far.

CHAPTER TWENTY-EIGHT

It was almost dawn. I stared up through the holes in the canvas and glimpsed the stars. "Are you awake?"

"No, I'm fast asleep," whispered Lorene.

She gave me a jab in the ribs. "Hey!"

I felt her soft, warm skin against mine. "How will Carlos get Maria away from the Savianos?"

"And he's still going on about his wife ..."

I'd felt a terrible, all-consuming remorse on one hand and a wonderful glow on the other.

She uncoiled herself from my arms and moved away, "Carlos and his family will be her immediate body-guards. So, as long as Charles Saviano is unaware that the Carlos is against the marriage, he might have a chance to move her somewhere for a while."

"How?" I whispered.

"That is his problem. But I believe he will try."

"Me persuading Maria to come home has got to be the easiest way for Carlos to stop the whole union, right?"

"Probably," said Lorene, putting her clothes on.

"But things have changed," I whispered.

"Have they?"

There was a pause where I tried and failed to think of something to say.

"You need her to tell you how she really feels. Maybe you just need closure ..."

Lorene slipped out of the tent. The holes in the roof had turned a faint-blue as dawn eased across the sky.

I suddenly had a desperate need to pee, so I got up and got dressed, my thoughts drifting back to the night before. As I unfastened the ropes that tied the door, I realised that Willie's snoring had replaced the whir of the cicadas. It was almost as cold as Scotland, and I could taste sea salt in the air.

"Are you up too?"

It was Andy. He had his sleeping bag wrapped round him like a shawl.

"Where have you been?" I asked.

"Where do you think?" he moaned.

"Right," I said, suddenly spying the loo roll in his hand. "Where did you go?"

Andy pointed to an especially old-looking olive tree before throwing me the roll. "Behind there."

"Nice," I whispered.

"It wasn't really," he admitted. "It's only seven, so I'm going back to bed." He wriggled back into his tent, unfazed by Willie's trumpet-like snoring. He refastened his door.

I decided to head for a thick bush on the other side of the grove. On the way over I peered into Sasha's jeep but it was empty.

"Hey," said a voice. It was Lorene. She was holding a large holdall. "Sasha says she heard a helicopter. She's climbed up the hill a bit to see. I could do with your help," she waved the bag at me. "We need to pack the tents."

"Okay," I said, "but first I really have to *go see a man about a dog*." My stomach suddenly cramped.

"We all have to shit," she said, unfazed.

I forced a smile. Her comment was so European. They thought nothing of walking about bollock-naked in parks and beaches, whereas Glaswegians, quite happy to swear like troupers and knock the crap out of each other, found this kind of behaviour crass, even weird.

On the way back to the camp I saw Lorene undoing the guy ropes of our tent, so I mucked in, albeit resentful of Andy and Willie, who either ignored us or slept through the whole damn thing. I poked my head inside their tent and almost gagged on the stale, rancid air. "Ho! Mingers! Get up and get your tent packed away. We've got company.

I heard it now too. The far-off whirring of a helicopter. I looked back up towards the jeep and saw Sasha reversing it under a sandstone overhang. I finished rolling up our tent and followed Lorene. "What are the chances of getting something to eat?"

She reached into a rucksack and threw me a box of cereal bars. "That's as good as it gets."

Sasha sprinted out from the overhang to meet us. "They on their way."

"Maria?" I asked.

"No," said Sasha, "Galdini's men. Carlos says they are coming."

The sound of the helicopter grew louder.

Lorene pointed to Andy and Willie's tent. "Go and hurry them up, Ian. Quickly!"

I ran back towards their tent and shouted on Andy. Willie was still inside. "Get him out of there, now!"

A few moans and grunts later Willie staggered out into the fragile light. "It's fuckin' freezing."

"Come on," I shouted over my shoulder. The helicopter was almost on us. "Pull the tent down and drag it under that tree. Never mind the fuckin' pegs, Andy."

We'd just made it under the cover of the old tree when the helicopter eased over our field. Olives and dead leaves began raining down on our heads like confetti.

Through the canopy, I glimpsed a black helicopter with a red line along it. The side door was open and two men were sitting on the sill. They both had an arm through some netting while their guns poked out of the opening.

I crouched and waited, but it moved on, banking left over the next field and then the next again. The three of us sprinted a further fifty yards to the overhang and the jeep.

"We lucky," said Sasha, "they don't have infrared on board."

"How do you know?" asked Andy.

"They would not wait for daylight if had infrared," she answered.

Andy was just about to say something else but she held up her hand for silence.

Now we could hear another jeep coming down the track into our field.

Sasha and Lorene clipped their magazines into place and lay down in the long grass at the edge of the overhang.

We tucked ourselves in beside the jeep.

"Who is it?" whispered Andy.

"Shut up," barked Willie.

The jeep, an old beat-up Land Rover, threw a trail of dust up behind it as it drew nearer.

Sasha fired the first shot.

"Fuck!" yelped Andy, ducking down.

Lorene fired a second shot and the Land Rover smacked into one of the olive trees. Steam belched out of the radiator grille.

We waited a moment or two to see if there was any movement inside the Land Rover and then got up.

Gingerly, Willie, Andy and myself wandered across the grove after the girls.

Sasha and Lorene, their weapons still trained on the Land Rover, moved in and quickly opened the doors.

The driver was slouched across the steering wheel, a neat hole in his forehead. The passenger, a boy no older than eighteen, had a wound to his throat. He was still alive and choking horribly.

"They are Galdini's men," said Sasha, in a hateful tone.

"He's only a boy," I whispered.

Lorene shook her head bitterly. "He will die."

On hearing this, the boy's eyes began streaming with tears.

"Look," said Sasha. She pointed down at the two submachine guns lying at the boy's feet. "They came here to find us and kill us."

After coughing and spluttering on his own blood for a moment the boy raised an accusing finger at us. "I... I know you."

We all stared at each other and then back at the boy who, by now, was dead. His mouth was open and his eyes cloudy.

I stared at Willie for a long moment. "Did you know him?"

"Did I fuck," said Willie, moving back from the Land Rover.

"He had Scottish accent," said Sasha, "like the smelly one." She nodded at Willie.

"Piss off. I didn't know him, alright!" Willie wandered off obviously annoyed at all of us.

"He did sound as if he was Scottish," I agreed.

"But he looks Italian," said Andy.

"So what?" I said. "There are plenty of Italians in Scotland."

"He was choking on his own blood. So how can we be sure where the fuck he was from?" said Andy.

Sasha lifted a mobile from the driver's blood-soaked pocket. "I bet if we dial the last number, it will be helicopter."

But the helicopter had moved on and we began to pull the

man and the boy from the wrecked Land Rover.

"Take jeep and bodies over there," said Sasha. She pointed to the overhang.

"Surely these two will be missed," I said, pointing down at the bodies.

"Not straight away," said Sasha, "and now with wedding tomorrow, you need see your Maria today, or too late."

I caught Lorene's attention after a while and talked quietly to her beneath one of the trees. "I've been thinking."

"Yes?" she prompted.

"Why are we trying to stop the two clans coming together now? I mean, I know that from my point of view, I understand what Maria is all about now. I understand what I'm all about. Why should we help the Azuni family?"

Lorene checked the sights on her rifle. "We are alive right now because the Azuni family have decided they have a need for you. It makes sense to let this play out. You need to talk to Maria."

I bit my bottom lip and nodded slowly. "Of course," I said.

Sasha whistled and waved us all back to the overhang.

"What's wrong, Sasha?" asked Lorene. Andy and Willie had parked the jeep beside Sasha's and put the bodies in the back.

"Carlos is on his way," she said.

"With Maria?" I asked

"With Maria," she answered.

CHAPTER TWENTY-NINE

I felt my throat tighten at the very mention of Maria's name. Sasha was talking into her mobile again, nodding every couple of seconds and closing her eyes from time to time. She pointed to Andy and Willie, then motioned to Lorene. "You three must stay with jeep and dead people."

"That's not going to happen," said Lorene.

Sasha clipped her phone shut and stared hard at Lorene. "The meeting will be down there, by sea. Why you want make difficult?"

"I don't want to make it difficult, Sasha, it's just that I must continue to do my job." She pointed a long slender finger in my direction. "I am paid to keep him safe."

"He be safe," Sasha insisted. "And who pay you anyway? Carlos?"

I could see that this was causing Sasha great distress. "Look," I said, "couldn't Lorene be there but out of sight?"

"If Carlos see her, I get in trouble," said Sasha.

"He won't see me," promised Lorene.

With this last-minute piece of negotiation, we began our trek to the shore. Andy and Willie were both happy to hide in the overhang with the vehicles, although Andy had his reservations about the dead bodies.

As I walked closer to the sound of the sea my stomach began to churn with nerves. Lorene had disappeared into the undergrowth and Sasha was leading the way through a sandy corridor of evergreens.

"You look scared," she said over her shoulder.

"This is going to be weird," I mumbled.

"It was your wife who asked meet you in this place," she said.

We climbed up a steep incline and then wavered on the crest of a tufted dune. The sea was a deep aqua marine and there was a sickle-shaped slice of sand curving away from us. The breeze was warm and it ruffled the back of Sasha's short hair. She turned to face me and smiled but my attention was fixed on the beach below us. Everything was flooding back. "This is it," I muttered.

"Is what?" said Sasha.

"It's Dead Dog Beach," I said, slowly walking down the dune. "It's where we met, where I proposed…"

"Is nice place to see wife again, no?" said Sasha, her smile widening.

"But it's quiet. This was a busy beach ten years ago," I said.

"Is beach for turtles now," said Sasha, "not dead dogs, silly man."

"You mean it's protected?"

"Is protected, yes," said Sasha, "by Lorene too, I think," she added in a whisper, her eyes fixing on the horizon.

I looked around for any sign of Lorene but, of course, there was nothing.

"There," said Sasha., shading her eyes.

At the southern end of the beach, I could see two people walking along the shore line. The tallest of the two spotted us and pointed towards an old abandoned beach-bar. It was a basic wooden structure with the remnants of some palm leaves on the roof. I was sure I remembered the place.

"Is her?" asked Sasha.

"I …" My eyes were drying out in a southerly mistral breeze, my mind was cluttered.

When we reached the circular beach-bar I paused for a moment and peered inside. The wooden panelling was grey with age and a row of stranded bottle clips ran along a metal gantry, orange with rust.

"Ian?"

The voice came from the back of the bar.

Sasha tapped me on the shoulder. "I go with Carlos. Leave you in peace wis crazy wife."

I held my breath in anticipation.

Carlos edged out of the shadows, a pair of reflective shades set above his pronounced cheekbones. "You have thirty minutes," he said. "I managed to convince Charles Saviano that Maria would be safer on the move with me."

"But you said an hour," I protested.

"Twenty-nine minutes and counting. No more," he said in a

low gravelly voice.

I watched him wander off across Dead Dog Beach with Sasha, the blue sea racing up the flat sand towards their fresh footprints.

I stared back into the gloom of the bar. "Maria?"

And then she walked out into the dappled light, her face as beautiful as it had been that first day. "You came," she said.

My tongue had just stuck itself to the roof of my mouth.

"You were told you not to," she added.

Her hair was different. Bobbed and straight, it shone like a raven's wing. "You didn't really explain," I said.

"I couldn't," she said, her voice slipping into a familiar, argumentative tone.

"Look," I said. "I know our marriage was a sham but I'm not going to do the 'tit for tat' thing here. This isn't about scoring points. It's about us. We spent ten years together."

"And I knew all along that it had to end, that's why we made the pact."

I looked at her long and hard. Her tone had eased back a notch to cold and calculated. I couldn't believe she could just forget everything. "Maria, it's me …"

"And this is me," she said. "For the first time you know who I am, where I've come from, what I'm part of."

"You are part of me," I said.

Maria closed her eyes and exhaled.

I'd never felt so scared. Everything hung in the balance and now I didn't know which way I wanted this to play. "Do you even know this Franco Galdini?" I whispered.

"I've known him since I was five."

"And Carlos?" I broached.

"We were childhood sweethearts," she answered.

"And now?"

"And now I must do what I promised," said Maria. "I have to do to maintain the peace."

"Has Carlos spoken to you about what he wants?" I could tell by her confused expression that he hadn't.

"What do you mean?" she said.

"Ask him," I snapped. I felt myself getting angry but I managed to hold it back. "You must have some trace of affection for me, some glimmer of love, somewhere …" My voice broke and I had to clear my throat.

"Of course," she said. Maria pointed at the beach. "When I said yes on this beach, ten years ago, I knew what I was doing. I had my instructions. And it was easy at first because you were such an arsehole, but–"

"Thanks a bunch," I interrupted.

"But then I got used to you."

"For fuck's sake, Maria. You got 'used to me'?"

"That's why I wanted you to read the postcards," she said. "My feelings changed. I went from feeling nothing, to feeling sorry, to feeling something … but it's not enough."

"That guy Carlos is a murderer," I said, thinking about the way he dispatched Fred.

"He is a businessman," she corrected.

"Jesus, do you know about Lorene?"

"I should. I hired her."

I held my breath. "You …" I now began to wonder if last night had been paid for too. "For fuck's sake. You think you can control everything but …"

Maria tilted her head, as if sensing something but then she said, "I knew you would need protection. I might think you are a self-centred arse, but I don't want you dead."

Her expression darkened. "I need to go."

In a low trembling whisper, I said, "What kind of manipulating monster are you, Maria?"

"Fuck off, Ian," she snapped.

I felt the tendrils of rage and frustration pushing their way to the surface again. "Why did you even agree to meet me today? Why–"

"I owe you Ian," she interrupted.

"You could have saved me a whole lot of shit if you'd just told me about Carlos and Franco and your father before now."

"Don't make this any more difficult than it is, Ian," she said.

"So why did you give me the key?"

Maria looked confused.

"Why do you think? It was like giving you back our wedding ring." She gave me a disdainful glance before staring out over the sand. "It was symbolic."

"It might have been more than that."

"All that judges shit is just that: shit. Carlos thought his father was trying to give him something, help him, but he was wrong. The old man died on this beach and so did his secrets."

I didn't know what to say.

Maria continued to stare out across the beach where our lives had, ten years before, become so inextricably entwined. I reached for her hand but she pulled it away and bowed her head.

"So, this is it?" I said. "You're just going to give up on your life with me? Join forces with these sick bastards?"

"I love my father," said Maria.

"Your father is a fuckin' monster!" I snapped.

Maria slapped me across the face and walked out into the sunshine.

I stood, stunned for a moment, before staggering out after her. I could see Carlos talking to Sasha about a hundred yards further along the beach. I wondered about Lorene. Had she seen Maria hit me? Had she known all along that Maria had hired her? Was she torn between protecting me and protecting her paymaster? Had Maria actually paid Lorene to have sex with me?

"Look, Ian," said Maria, turning to face me, "I did grow to care for you... Still do, in a way, but …"

I ran over the sand and caught her arm. "If you really love Carlos, why are you going to marry Franco?" I said.

"It's our way," she said, flicking my hand away.

"Who are you afraid of, Maria? Your father? Antonio Galdini? Carlos?"

Maria dried her eyes with the back of her sleeve, smudging her mascara. Black, clown-like tear tracks traced down over her flawless complexion. "I'm afraid for my people, my family …"

"Who are you, Maria?"

She stared hard at me. "Who are you? You've changed. It's like you're a different guy."

"I've been shot at, almost rammed off a road, forced to dig my own grave and, get this Maria … I watched the love of your life, Carlos Azuni, cut Fred Marvin's hand off before throwing him off a ferry into the sea. Of course, I've fucking changed. I'm probably going to need therapy for the rest of my life."

"Fred Marvin was the Galdini's eyes and ears in Scotland."

"Well, now he's fish food."

She drew a heavy sigh and nodded across at Carlos who nodded back.

"Carlos is a good man at heart, Ian. I think he just wanted to see if I had feelings for you."

"Jesus." Ian rolled his eyes.

"Carlos wanted to give me the chance to go home with you–if I really wanted to."

"So, why don't you?" barked Ian. "Why don't you come home right now?"

"I can't," whispered Maria.

"Carlos wants you to come home with me. He doesn't want things to change. I'm telling you, this is your last chance."

She stopped in her tracks and looked me straight in the eye. "This is way bigger than you, me or any Azuni."

I knew then that she was truly lost, a real Saviano. Just as ruthless as her father.

There was a shout from somewhere beyond the beach bar. We both ran back into the shadows.

Carlos and Sasha had begun running towards us, their guns drawn.

"Get down!" Sasha yelled ahead of her.

Back inside, we both ducked down behind the old bar.

Carlos skidded to a stop behind Sasha. "We have to go now," he said.

I felt the blood drain from my face as I watched Carlos grip Maria's hand. She pushed him away and almost spat her words. "This better not have been about you!"

Carlos gave Maria a puzzled glance. "We don't have time!" He caught my eye before he dashed out the door and I could tell he was raging. It had, after all, been my job to get Maria to call off the wedding, to keep the status quo. And I'd failed.

Sasha was still at my side. "So?" she asked, expectantly.

I returned her stare with glazed eyes. "I... I don't think I managed to convince her to come back."

"So now you go home and get on with life, no?" she said.

I was both taken aback and intrigued by her abruptness. "What was the point of all this?" I whispered.

"No time for 'point'," said Sasha. "More Galdini men coming. Saviano men too, I think. We run, hide."

A crack of gunfire sounded out over the pounding of the waves. The breeze became stronger and dark, ominous clouds slipped across the horizon. Any residual glamour or sunny memories that Dead Dog Beach may have held faded away for good. The place looked drab, unwelcoming and deserted.

Another shot rang out from further inland.

"They are in olive grove," said Sasha, adjusting her pack.

Ian looked back across the beach for Maria, but she was gone. "What about Willie and Andy?" he whispered.

"They hide, or maybe dead," said Sasha, nonplussed.

There was a click of a lock and then a familiar voice. "Are you okay, Ian?"

Lorene and Sasha faced each other in the gloom, poised, their fingers hovering, precariously, over damp triggers.

"Where were you?" I asked.

"Close enough," said Lorene.

"He sad," added Sasha.

My mouth opened and my shoulders dropped in exasperation. "Can we go?"

Sasha continued to update Lorene, "Maria... She say no."

Lorene squinted at me inquisitively as I made my way out of the bar. We all began to trot across the cold sand. Lorene soon took the lead.

"So, what now, Lorene?" I shouted after her.

She turned and shushed me.

"You're probably free to leave," I continued, in a slightly quieter voice.

"Not until I'm instructed to," she said, over her shoulder. She weaved between the dunes before, once more, finding the well-beaten track that led back to the olive grove.

Now we were off the beach, Lorene slowed us down. "We should split up."

I moved as close to Lorene as I could and said, "Maria is the one who hired you, but you probably knew that all along."

Lorene looked at me in horror. "What are you trying to say?"

"I ..." I instantly knew I'd really offended her.

Oblivious to my stupid comment, Sasha gave a brisk nod and moved away.

"Wait... What am I supposed to do now?" I asked.

"Stay here. You are bait!" said Sasha. "Like worm!" she added, slipping through a hedge.

When I looked round again I was alone on the single track road. Lorene was gone too and I could feel all the little pieces of hope I'd kept close to my heart beginning to melt away. Some settled in the pit of my stomach as kernels of self-loathing while others drifted up to my brain and began to burrow themselves into my self-esteem.

I was a grown man, yet I could feel myself welling up as I walked a little further into the grove; more alone than ever.

"Stop there!" a voice called out in stilted English.

Three swarthy-skinned men in suits emerged from behind some trees, their guns trained.

Another four appeared to my left.

I squinted beyond them, towards the cave where I knew Andy and Willie had hidden.

The tallest of the seven smiled wryly and said, "They surrendered like cowards." He turned to the rest of the men. "Get him in the jeep."

I waited for a burst of gunfire from Sasha or Lorene, but it never came. Anxiously, I stared hard at the tall man. "Who do you work for?"

My question was answered with a fist to the side of my head. Black lumps of nothingness clogged my thoughts. I could taste blood. My legs buckled.

CHAPTER THIRTY

A cold breeze made me shiver as I tried to open my eyes. My clothes felt damp and there was a piece of blue twine tied tightly around my wrist. I tried to get up but another length of rope fixed me, like an umbilical cord, to a stark stone wall.

"Happy Christmas, dick breath."

I peered into the dim recesses of the bare room until I eventually picked out Willie hunkered down in a corner.

"Your fuckin' wife paid you a visit while you were out cold," he said.

"Maria?"

"No, Gina Lollobrigida. Who the fuck do you think? She was with her new man; they checked your knots and fucked off again."

"New man?"

"Franco Galdini. And get this, we've all met him already."

"Where?"

"Remember the Italians on the Dover ferry? The guy I smacked first?"

"That was Franco Galdini?"

"Aye," said Willie, "and he popped me one on the way out. Said he owed me."

I could see some blood at the side of Willie's mouth.

"Where's Andy?" I asked in a hoarse whisper.

Before answering, Willie edged closer and pushed a bucket of water towards me with his foot. "There's a ladle in there. Have a drink. As far as Andy's concerned, I haven't got a fucking clue. They came for us as soon as you disappeared with the two birds. Knew exactly where to find us. They were going to pop us right there and then until I told them I was Uncle Fred's nephew. I reckoned I had nothing to lose, and it paid off. They were Galdini men. They knew about the Marvins, about Uncle Fred being thrown from the ferry."

"So they didn't blame us for that?" I asked.

"No way. They knew it was Carlos Azuni's work. Said it was a bit of a trademark of his."

"So Carlos must chuck people off the ferry for his boss on a regular basis then?"

"Looks like it," sneered Willie. "The bastard."

"So, Maria just came in and made sure I was tied up nice and tight?" I pressed.

"Pretty much," answered Willie. "Franco tested your knots while she was babbling in fuckin' Italian."

"I don't get it." I pulled on the nylon rope and cursed. A red welt on my wrist was stinging like hell. The Galdinis, Azunis and Savianos must all be in place for the wedding, but where was Andy? "Did you see Lorene or Sasha?"

Willie narrowed his eyes. "I only saw the Russian whore. She covered the door while Maria and Franco came in to see you."

"Do you think this is the wedding venue?" I said, in a shaky voice.

Willie spat onto the dirt floor. "It's a bit of a shit hole if it is."

A crack of gunfire echoed out above us.

Willie grunted and then stood up rubbing his wrist. "They never checked my knots, the stupid fuckers." He moved over to me and began working on the twine that held me fast.

I tried to shake the pain away from my wrist, but it stung like mad as my hand underwent the painful process of refill. Blood seeped back under my battered watch, into the starved capillaries and arteries. But I knew that I would never be able to shift the feeling of betrayal that crawled over me like a stinging rash. "She's going to stay here," I pronounced, randomly. "She's not going to come home. I spoke to her on the beach."

Willie looked both confused and unimpressed. "What did you expect, you dick?"

"And you haven't seen Lorene?"

"No."

I shouldn't have doubted Lorene. Now remorse was replacing that feeling of betrayal. I'd acted too quickly, and now I'd probably lost the only woman who actually got me.

Shouts erupted in the corridor outside our cell.

Willie pulled me flat against the wall behind the door and handed me a long piece of wood. "Even if it's your fucked-up wife. Hit her hard and run."

I felt sick. "No way."

The door squeaked open and two men burst into the room.

Willie let the first one creep in, but caught the second man on the back of the head with a piece of masonry. The first man turned but before he could fix his aim, I smashed his nose with a perfectly executed forward kick. The man issued a nasal shriek and dropped the gun.

Willie stared down at the two men and said, "So, you can actually do karate?"

"I was the Scottish Junior Champion two years in a row."

More shots rang out.

"Sounds like there's a fuckin' war going on up there," said Willie. "We need to find Andy."

I followed Willie out into the dark corridor and then up a set of stone stairs that shimmered with damp. "Those guys must have been sent down to get us."

"Or kill us," added Willie.

Willie and I both crouched down and waited. I held my breath, peering into the darkness. There was another blast of gunfire.

"It doesn't seem like their big truce is going to hold out, wedding or not," I said. "Where are we?"

"They had a hood over my head, but we're in some kind of castle," said Willie.

Another exchange of gunfire shook clumps of lime mortar out of the old stone walls.

We turned a corner and stepped into a bright circular room lined with heavy tapestries. Willie pointed to a large panelled door. "That is our way out," he said.

"Wait, we can't leave without Andy."

"I know, but where do we start?" said Willie.

The panelled door we'd been looking at suddenly burst inward and a hail of bullets rattled across the room.

We ducked behind a stack of tables.

"Shit, shit, shit," hissed Willie.

Bullets pinged off of the stone walls behind us as people poured into the room.

"Shut the fucking door!" yelled an old man. "Those

treacherous bastards!"

"Franco!" Yelled a very familiar voice.

I eased up until I could see over the tables. I had to be sure.

The panelled door was slammed shut as another hail of bullets rattled across the room.

"Was that ...?" whispered Willie, jerking his thumb in the general direction of the intruders.

I nodded and mouthed the name, 'Maria'.

"Now what do we do?" said another voice, in a Glaswegian accent.

I watched Willie's eyes bulge in disbelief before I heard him whisper, "Is that fuckin' Andy talking?"

More shouts clamoured behind the massive panelled door and a velvet window curtain to our left was suddenly pulverized in a torrent of gunfire.

"Fuck, fuck, fuck," said Willie in an even more anxious whisper.

Someone out in the middle of the room fell to the floor with a grunt.

"Papa!"

I squinted through the tables to see who'd spoken.

There, in the middle of the circular room, three men and a woman knelt round an old, frail-looking man.

I recognised Andy, and Maria straight away. A third man, balding and dressed in a black cassock, was holding a gold cross above the old man's face. Then I saw him. The football supporter from the Dover ferry, Franco Galdini, the man whom Maria was going to marry.

I focussed in on Maria's expression. Her face was full of false sympathy. I knew this look. It was the look I'd often received when I relayed the weekly calls about possible gigs that never quite came off or possible song interest that never really materialised – 'pies in the sky' that always came to nothing. I'd always known that she had other, more important things on her mind, like the bills, the dog, decorating, dinner ... But I never once suspected that she might have been thinking about the fucking Sardinian Mafia, Carlos Azuni–the love of her life, Franco Galdini–the man she would have to marry, or the four dead judges–who, if they were ever found, would land the Galdini and Saviano bosses in jail for life. As my mind cleared I tried to work out the scene in front of me.

Why was Andy acting like he knew them all? Who was the old man that had fallen?

"Antonio!" said Maria, staring down. Her face was still brimming with false concern.

I stood up.

"What the fuck are you doing?" hissed Willie.

CHAPTER THIRTY-ONE

The priest, dented in prayer, muttered a few words in Italian that floated up into the wooden rafters above.

Franco screamed out in anguish and fell to the floor while Maria slowly rose to her feet, her face full of disbelief. "Ian?" she said.

Andy looked shaken, unsure what to say or do. "I... You see, I was ..."

"You were fuckin' what? You little piece of shit," said Willie.

"It's Antonio Galdini," gasped Andy.

I recognized the old man now. I'd seen him talking to Fred Marvin outside the café in Rome. I thought back to my first kiss with Lorene.

"You treacherous little fuck," continued Willie.

"No. You've got it all wrong," said Andy.

Maria stared straight at us and said, "Andy's mother was an Azuni."

"What the fuck?" hissed Willie.

Andy stared down at the floor.

"The gigs?" I spat.

"Arranged by Carlos," said Andy.

"He's in big trouble," said Maria, "Neither Carlos nor Andy had any right helping you."

"And the postcards?" I blurted.

"That was Carlos's idea," said Andy, his face glowing crimson.

"What about Uncle Fred?" snapped Willie.

"I told you not to get him involved," muttered Andy.

Everything poured back into my head. Andy being there just as Maria left me at the anniversary dinner. The way he'd come home with me and got me to embark on a quest for Maria. Carlos appearing at our door with his mock warning. Probably to make Andy look more believable. Jesus. The band getting back together, the gigs ... "So you're one of Maria's fuckin' Azuni servants?"

The question hung unanswered in the muggy air as the priest continued to mutter over the old man's corpse.

Andy, still shaking, cowered away as Willie moved closer.

Franco Galdini stood up, his face full of rage. "Your family will pay for this."

"Wait,' said Maria, "It was an accident. Your father would still want this to go ahead."

Franco stormed over to the panelled door and pushed it open. "Where are you, you bunch of fucking cowards?"

"Franco! Come away from the door!" yelled Maria. She ran forward and yanked him back just as another torrent of lead peppered the room. The curtains swished and danced for a few seconds before it fell silent again.

Crouching down with the rest of us, the priest pointed at Franco and then at Maria. "She's right. You must marry her now! You can still stop this war."

Maria and Franco stared into each other's eyes.

I watched them, trying to gauge their feelings for each other. They hovered inches away from a tattered velvet curtain, their faces covered in beads of sweat.

"It's the only way," pressed Maria.

"Don't do it," I moaned. "Look what's happening here. The two families are still firing at each other. There is too much resentment."

Franco closed his eyes for a moment and then said, "We need a witness." He pointed at me. "You can all take part in the ceremony. Once they know we are married, it will all stop."

I shook my head in disbelief. "You really think so?"

Willie caught Andy by the throat.

"Leave him, Willie," snapped Maria. "Everyone here, apart from Ian and the priest, has come from a family steeped in blood."

Willie drew back.

The priest nodded sternly and began searching through his bible. "I can do it right now."

I looked down at Antonio. "He was your enemy, Maria, a mass murderer," I said.

Franco moved forward.

Maria caught his arm. "I need my father to be here."

"Why didn't your father control his men?" I asked, pointing at the door.

"It only took one shot and both sides let loose," said Maria.

"It just kicked off," said Andy. "Carlos tried to calm them down but..."

"It was one of our guys," said Franco. "Charles Saviano killed the guy's mother."

"Too much," I protested. "This is all too much."

"The families lived side by side, in peace, for years," said Franco. He had dropped down beside his dead father again, his eyes full of sorrow.

"We were best friends when we were kids," said Maria. She was teasing Franco's thick hair. "But then the Savianos and the Galdinis fell out over land and the killing started. Franco was forbidden to see me. We didn't know we were supposed to hate each other. It just got worse and worse. For years and years."

"Where did Carlos fit in?" I said, interested to see if Maria would betray her real feelings for her supposed bodyguard to Franco.

"We are only there to support and help the Savianos," said Andy.

"We?" I still couldn't get my head round Andy. It had all gone very quiet since the last hail of bullets.

There was a loud creak as the big panelled door swung inward.

Franco aimed his gun and then lowered it again. "Mr Saviano."

Charles Saviano was in his seventies but still very well turned out. A neat suit covered his lithe frame and he walked tall, his back straight, his eyes fixed on me.

Carlos Azuni was at his side, dragging a body into the room. Behind them, an assortment of men bundled into the room.

Carlos placed the corpse on the floor beside Antonio. "This one started the firing first. A Galdini." He bit the inside of his cheek and shook his head at Franco. "If your father could have only kept his henchmen in order—"

"That's enough, Carlos!" snapped Charles.

Franco clenched his fists but Maria steadied him.

"Isn't this a turn up for the books?" said Charles. "You," he stabbed my chest with a long withered finger, "are a very stupid man."

"You can say that again."

Franco pointed down at his dead father, "Who fired that shot?"

"That would have been me," replied Charles indignantly. "One of the bullets must have gone straight through him." He flicked his fingers at the dead Galdini henchman.

"Dad! You could have hit me!" Maria caught Franco's arm for a second time.

"You should have stuck to the plan, Maria, instead of worrying about *that self-obsessed idiot*." Charles pointed at me.

"I'm actually sorry we killed Antonio. I would have loved him to see this. To witness his only son marrying into the Savianos. To see Franco become Franco Galdini Saviano... No wonder he tried to stop it."

"He didn't try to stop it," barked Franco. "He knew it was the only way to bring this war between us to a close."

Charles grunted disdainfully. "You don't have to tell me about the war. About the casualties ..." He peered over the heads of his men before saying, "Is everyone in the room? I want every Galdini and Saviano inside."

There was a series of commands issued in Italian before one of the Saviano men nodded and closed the heavy door.

"Perhaps we should just perform the ceremony right here and now, before any more blood is spilled," suggested the priest.

Charles smiled to himself before addressing the room. "It is time for a new order. A new beginning. Between us, we control over half the casinos in Europe. We have people in high places in nearly every government. And now we have every top member of both families all in the one spot." Charles looked at every face in turn. "All guns and weapons on the middle table," he ordered. He turned to Franco. "You are the head of the Galdini family now, which makes the union even more powerful. The wedding will go ahead."

The priest reopened his bible and ushered the assorted henchmen, Scotsmen and assassins into some kind of order.

I still couldn't stop thinking about Lorene. What I had said to her... I kept imagining her face, as she turned and walked away for the last time. It was crazy. Maria was going to go ahead and marry Franco and all I was worried about was what Lorene thought of me. True to type–I'd been an arsehole … again.

"We need a best man," announced the priest.

I stepped forward and after a long sigh said, "That should probably be me."

"What?" said Andy.

"Don't even speak to me, Andy, you manipulating little shit."

Carlos Azuni's face was red with anger. It was pretty obvious that Carlos and Andy had pretty high hopes that I'd change Maria's mind. Keep the status quo. Well, they weren't going to manipulate me this time.

Sasha placed her gun on the big table and Franco followed suit.

As I walked to the front of the group to take up my position, Willie coughed loudly. He gave me a double wink which meant 'he wanted to shag someone' in band speak. I was confused. Then I saw him nod at the big tapestry on the wall.

I mouthed the word 'What?'.

Maria suddenly ruffled her hair and turned to the priest. "We need a ring."

I looked down at her left hand and sighed. "You can recycle that one."

Maria looked at me incredulously.

"The ring served *us* well."

"You think?" sighed Maria, already slipping it from her finger.

"Yeah... I think. It might give you another ten years."

Grim-faced, Franco let Maria place the ring in the palm of his right hand.

The priest began to read a passage from the 'wedding at Cana', but cut straight to the vows when Charles Saviano gave him a look.

I felt physically sick as I watched the scene unfold. Like some cuckold groom, I felt both disgust and strange relief. When it came to the part where the priest said, "Is there anyone present who has lawful impediment?" the tension in the circular room was unbearable.

"In that case," continued the priest.

"Wait!" said a low, yet forceful voice.

Franco and Maria peered at the onlookers.

"Father?" said Franco.

Charles Saviano and his men bristled. They shuffled aside to make room for Franco.

A few yards away, Antonio Galdini was getting to his feet.

I blinked. I was sure he was dead…

The old man grunted. "I always wear Kevlar now."

"Is good stuff," added Sasha, rather unhelpfully.

"And you didn't tell me?" moaned Franco.

"I don't have to tell you everything," snapped Antonio. He nodded disdainfully at Charles Saviano. "Thought you'd got me, Charles? Eh?"

"No. That's…"

"Not important now," finished Antonio, one hand on his chest. He flicked his other hand at the astonished priest. "Keep going!"

The priest asked Franco to give him the ring and then he blessed it before saying, "Do you, Franco Galdini, take Maria to be your lawful, married wife?"

"I do," said Franco.

I stared hard at the side of Maria's face while she listened to the priest asking her the reciprocal question. But then she said it…

"I do."

Tears rolled down over her cheeks onto her grubby roll-neck sweater, but I could tell that my 'wife' was no longer mine. She really looked like she wanted this, as if she'd always wanted this.

Willie moved in beside me and whispered, "Her loss. Now, keep an eye on the tapestry…"

Andy tried to shuffle in beside Willie and myself, but Willie stopped him dead with a curt, "Fuck off, traitor."

Andy, crestfallen, eased away again.

I shouldn't have, but part of me felt sorry for Andy. We'd been through so much together. He'd been as true to me as any other fucker in my life. Yes, he probably had his own agenda, but who didn't. Everyone has their own reasons for doing stuff, even Willie.

Willie tugged on my coat, pulling me away from the celebrations—and my thoughts.

Gingerly edging back with Willie, I saw the two old men,

Antonio Galdini and Charles Saviano, looking grimly at each other. They both looked beaten, yet quietly relieved. The guns on the middle table lay untouched, their obsequious owners, now offering outstretched hands to men who were enemies only moments before.

"Time to leave," whispered Willie.

"How?" I whispered back.

CHAPTER THIRTY-TWO

Again, Charles Saviano called for silence. "Now that we are all one big family, it is time to cement the new leadership."

Antonio nodded, giving Charles a knowing smile.

Willie pulled me further away from Maria.

"Everyone here has played a major part in getting us this far," said Charles. He pointed down at the dead Galdini henchman, "Well, most of you. And," he continued, "as in any merger, there is always a need for some change, some restructure."

Everyone was beginning to look a little uneasy.

"As you came in, Carlos gave some of you a small grey wedding keepsake. A gift from both families."

A few men held these up proudly.

"Did you notice Carlos do that?" I asked Willie.

Andy, a desperate look on his face had pushed in beside us again. "Keep low," he managed to say, before Willie shoved him away.

"What's that supposed to mean?" I whispered to Willie.

"We have picked our new leadership team," continued Antonio. He produced a metal canister. "I suggest, if you have one, that you open your gifts now."

With this, he rolled the canister into the middle of the room and pulled a clear mask from his pouch.

Carlos swung a rucksack from his shoulder and handed Maria and Franco a mask.

"No!" protested Maria.

The canister immediately oozed a thick trail of noxious white smoke.

"Put the masks on now!" yelled Antonio.

Sasha hit the floor and began crawling towards the door, lizard fashion.

Apart from the few who had masks, the rest of the mob, too busy trying to reach their guns, knocked each other over in blind panic before coughing and dropping to their knees.

Willie and I, now seeing what Andy meant, instantly copied Sasha. My lungs were constricting. My skin burning. I could just see the door through the white swirling mist. The circular room was full of the screams and coughs of the dying. A shot rang out and then there was the clatter of metal on the hard floor.

Through a foggy haze, I heard Charles Saviano's muffled shout. "Wait until the smoke clears then shoot any survivors!"

Beside the heavy tapestry, I felt a hand pull at my arm and someone thumped down next to me. My eyes were burning.

A mask was shoved over my mouth and a voice said, "Take two deep breaths."

Everything was spinning.

I drew the dry oxygen deep into my lungs and tried to focus on my rescuer, but another set of hands was already dragging me out of the room. I landed in a heap as a door was slammed shut behind me, the sounds of shouting suddenly more muffled and unworldly.

"I don't think much of your in-laws," said Lorene.

My thoughts were still muggy. "They're not... in-laws," I wheezed, "any more."

Willie was lying beside Sasha. He panicked and tried to catch her with a punch, but she caught his wrist and said, "Like you, I never got wedding present mask."

Willie rolled away from Sasha. "I saw Lorene behind the tapestry a few moments before it all kicked off," he explained.

"And I saw you seeing her," added Sasha. "We go now, if you want live."

I tried to get to my feet but a wave of nausea gripped me and I threw up.

Willie dragged me further away from the sounds of screaming and gunfire and soon we were trundling down a steep set of stairs while I coughed and retched.

Sasha and Lorene ran ahead. A door creaked open and a slice of sunlight flashed up the stairwell towards us. I had to shut my eyes.

"Wait!"

We all stopped dead.

"It's me."

Andy skidded to a halt a few yards behind us.

"What's your game, Andy? How could you fucking lie to us like that?" I squinted across at our wayward drummer. I tried to make out his expression, but Andy said nothing. He just kept stumbling along towards us.

Sasha hauled him the last few yards out into the courtyard and Willie caught hold of him, slamming him against a wall.

Andy's eyes were streaming. "I didn't have any say in it," he panted.

Willie drew back from him, like he had the plague.

"You were just following orders, Andy, is that it?" I said. "It didn't matter that we were your friends, your band mates for years," I moaned.

"Only when it suited you," hissed Andy.

"Shut up," snapped Willie.

"Following orders," I repeated. "I don't believe it."

Lorene caught my arm. "Do you think I was following orders last night?"

Everyone gave her a puzzled glance except for me. Head hung low, I squinted up at her and said, "No. I was an arsehole for even thinking it."

"Correct," said Lorene.

I tried to catch hold of her hand but she drew it away.

"If you two lovebirds have finished…" said Willie, pointing at an abandoned jeep, "we can maybe make a move."

"Or do you want to stay–try and win wife back again?" added Sasha.

I smiled. "We should go."

"Good decision," shouted Lorene.

We piled into the jeep and Sasha started it up. "It not have much petrol. Maybe we go in next one." She began climbing out of the driver's seat, but Willie pulled her back in. "Just go!"

As the jeep sputtered forward in the courtyard, I could see a large pair of rickety doors barring our way.

"The gates are shut!" moaned Andy.

"Keeping going," urged Lorene.

"Hold on!" added Sasha, stamping down on the accelerator.

Bullets were slamming into the jeep from behind, tearing through the weathered doors ahead of us.

I braced as we hit the gates.

The jolt knocked us back into our seats. A blizzard of shards and splinters tumbled ahead of us and then we were through, bouncing onto a sandy track.

Still moving fast, the jeep spluttered loudly.

"She's running out of fuel!" roared Lorene.

"I tell you this already!" snapped Sasha.

I felt another jolt beneath us and yelled out as the jeep dropped down on one side and then rolled.

The sound of screeching metal filled my head as sand filled my mouth and stones tore at my skin. The air was forced from my lungs. My head cracked against something hard.

* * *

I woke to the cry of an eagle. I could see its broad tail fanned out against the thermals. It circled above me in a flawless, summer-blue sky.

On my back, on the sandy track, the jeep was gone. My arm was covered in blood. I could hear people walking towards me, two men talking in Italian, a woman weeping. My mouth was stuck shut, clogged with foul-tasting dust.

Disorientated and aching all over, I grunted and rolled onto my stomach. I was lying at the very edge of a bridge, inches away from a massive drop into a deep ravine.

The castle had been built on a giant, granite buttress. Set apart from the rest of the mountain, the narrow, umbilical bridge was the only connection to the outside world.

I tried to edge myself up enough to peer over the other side of the bridge but the pain in my arm forced me back down again. There was no sign of the jeep or any of its passengers.

Carlos Azuni was striding purposely towards me.

I squinted into the sunlight and caught sight of Maria behind him, Franco holding her back. "It's time to move on," he told her.

Carlos drew close to me and glowered down. "Yes, Ian. Franco is right. It's time." He pointed down at the gorge, a warm wind blowing clouds of fine sand over the muzzle of his gun.

"Wait!" I panted.

"Wait for what?"

The eagle above us cried out and Carlos glanced up. Still looking skyward, he said, in a low voice, "You failed, and the Azunis are screwed because Maria is now married to a Galdini."

I wondered if I was supposed to feel sorry for this murdering asshole. "You got a mask, right?"

"This time, I did," he replied.

I could hear Franco urging Carlos to hurry up. I couldn't see or hear anyone else. Feeling a kind of illogical belligerence, I looked up into Carlos's dark eyes and said, "Go ahead. Kill me if you think you can."

A puzzled look on his face, Carlos forced a heavy foot on my chest and placed the cold barrel of his rifle against my neck. "I should have thrown you into the sea with that treacherous fuck, Fred Marvin, you useless – Argh!"

Blood spurted over my face. I had to blink it out of my eyes.

Carlos began wailing above me.

I grunted and rolled away from the edge of the bridge.

"Fuck!" Carlos couldn't reach me.

A few yards away now, I squinted back and saw an eight-inch hunting knife. It had pinned his foot to the track.

Lorene pulled herself up onto the bridge, her snow-white fingers wrapped around the hilt of the knife.

Carlos had dropped his gun. He was roaring out in agony, teetering on the edge.

Swinging herself up onto the bridge, Lorene jerked the knife free and sliced through his hamstring.

Franco opened fire but Maria was screaming, pushing the barrel of his gun off its mark.

Carlos flailed his arms, cartwheeling backwards as he tumbled over Lorene. He screamed out Maria's name as he fell into the abyss, his pitch becoming higher and more frantic until his fall was interrupted by an outcrop far below.

We both watched him, his limbs torn away from his body as he juddered off the jagged sides of the deep ravine.

The eagle continued to circle above us, bleating out its chilling lament.

Franco pulled away from Maria, but Charles Saviano appeared and rushed forward before Lorene could get to her feet. He kicked Carlos's gun away and pressed the muzzle of his AK47 against the side of her face.

I swung a broken arm at him, but only partially made contact, yelling out in agony.

Charles spat into the sand and brought his gun back into position.

Lorene's eyes widened in anticipation before Saviano smiled and pulled the trigger.

Lorene jerked her head back out of the way but hit a rock and fell still.

I kicked at Saviano's ankle and the bullets tore a rut in the road between us.

Saviano cursed and then nodded with satisfaction.

Lorene lay still, her left ear oozing blood, her eyes closed.

I gasped. "No!"

Saviano was just about to fire again when Maria grabbed his elbow and yelled, "No! I won't let you."

Franco stood back with Antonio, who looked very grey.

I was shaking with a mixture of fear and exhaustion.

"You won't let me?" snapped Saviano. He slapped Maria hard across the face and watched her fall back. "You won't let me?" he repeated. "I'm your father!" He prodded his own chest with his finger, the gun trailing by his side.

Still trembling, I tried to roll further away. As if in slow motion, my mind replayed every postcard-reminder of my previous life. My fingers clawed at the blood-spattered sand and an inexplicable calmness washed over me. Like a new-born slipping into another incarnation, I saw fragments of my former life moving sluggishly towards a deep abyss. Spilling over into a lost infinity of forgotten existence. I felt ready... ready to die right there in the Sardinian sand. I wondered if the sand was the same sand I'd stood on all those years ago. Blown up into the mountains by the warm winds that rush in from the sea. Whisked up from Dead Dog Beach into the granite peaks and gorges, onto the very bridge where my life was going to end.

Maria was getting back to her feet, her bruised lips dripping crimson. She was crying.

I stared up into the dead eyes of the psychopath, Saviano. "What else are you going to do to her?" I whispered, weakly. "Your own daughter... You made her marry me, stay in exile for ten years to save your skin. And now you've made her marry Franco, when the only man she really loved was Carlos."

Charles looked puzzled.

"And now Carlos is dead," I continued. "What else are you going to do to her?"

I winced as I moved my legs into a kneeling position. "Let her go, Charles. Let Maria live her own life for once."

"Stop it, Ian," sighed Maria.

"Is this true?" Antonio almost spat out the words. "Were you in love with an Azuni, a servant to the clan?"

"They are not servants, father." She began sobbing. "Carlos was not a servant."

"Oh... you've spent too long away from Sardinia, from your responsibilities," hissed Charles.

I was desperately trying to spot Sasha or Willie, or even Andy, but they were nowhere in sight.

"You see, that's what I'm talking about," continued Charles, rolling his eyes, "Where is your backbone, Maria? This idiot has to die." He pointed straight at me.

Maria was standing right beside her father, her dark hair ruffling in the breeze.

I heard the eagle screech down at me in warning.

"Wait!" I pleaded.

"Wait for what?" snapped Charles. "Wait for you to go to the authorities and tell them everything?"

I felt my chest tighten. "I would never tell them where the four judges are buried," I whispered.

Charles kicked me in the ribs. "What the fuck did you say?"

"I know where the bodies are."

Charles shook his head. "No one knows that. Not even me. That secret died with his father." He pointed down into the gorge. "Carlos' father was the only man who knew."

Charles moved in closer. "Your fucking key... Dead Dog Beach... I know everything about it. We checked the locker long before you and your boy scouts took a look. Nothing... there was nothing in there. The old man was wrong. Delirious or something. He buried them. And he took the secret to his grave."

"No he didn't," I said.

Charles just laughed.

Maria stood like a zombie bride beside her father. A layer of dust covered her smart clothes and her complexion was lustreless. She looked drained and close to passing out.

Charles Saviano clicked another magazine into the AK47 and handed it to Maria. "You have to do it," he said. "Prove that you are a real Saviano. Put this mad dog out of his misery."

Maria stared at the gun in her hand for a long moment before slipping a delicate finger behind the trigger. "You want *me* to finish this?"

"Yes! You need to move on," said Saviano, his face brightening. His teeth far too white and perfect for his wizened face.

Maria swung the barrel in my direction. I couldn't read her face.

A single tear rolled down her cheek as she closed her eyes and pulled the trigger.

CHAPTER THIRTY-THREE

The eagle dived as the sound of gunfire screamed out over the ravine. It dropped like a stone, its wings tucked in tight. Flying past Maria, its feathers ruffled loudly as it chased the falling man down into the abyss. Maria began to sob.

"Drop the gun, Maria!"

Without looking to see who it was, Maria threw her gun over the side of the bridge and flopped down onto the blood-stained sand, her whole body shaking. "What have I done?" she whimpered.

Through a swirling cloud of dust, I could see Willie and Sasha walking towards them. Andy was there too. He had a gash on his arm and he was limping. I reached for Maria. I wanted to console her, but then Lorene was suddenly awake. She rolled to her feet, caught my hand and pulled me away.

"Lorene," I said, surprised to see her so lucid after her crack to the head.

She helped me up and walked me away from Maria, towards Willie and Sasha. "I'm fine," I said. "She doesn't have a gun any more. Besides, she wouldn't harm me."

Lorene drew back. "She's just shot her own father."

Irritated by Lorene's twisted logic, I broke away from her and staggered back towards Maria. As I knelt down to console her, I stared hard into her brown eyes. "You can break free of all this." My thoughts were muddled, my eyes stinging and clogged with dry Sardinian sand.

A jeep was driving away, down the steep winding road.

"Your new man and his father have just done a runner," said Willie.

"I killed my own father," said Maria, matter-of-factly. Her voice was monotone, free of all emotion.

"He was a monster, Maria," I said, briefly peering over the edge of the bridge.

They all gasped and stepped back as the eagle flew up from the gorge, a rabbit clutched tight in its talons. I was so close that I could see the rabbit's eyes. Black and bulging.

The sight of the bird and its wretched catch seemed to snap Maria back into reality. "I have to go," she mumbled. Everyone turned away from the ravine and stared hard at the cloud of dust in the distance. Franco's jeep was winding its way down the mountain track. A further four trucks were even further down the road.

Maria turned to Andy.

Lorene caught my hand and eased me away. "I think she will always be a Saviano."

Willie was just about to have a go at Andy but Sasha held him back.

"And Andy?" I asked Lorene.

"He always was an Azuni. You just didn't know."

Sasha was helping Willie dress a small cut on his arm. "Now what you do, Mrs Galdini?"

Maria looked perplexed for a moment before saying, "This is my home. There are things to sort out." She pointed to the row of jeeps and trucks and handed Andy a key.

"Fuck me," said Willie.

Andy smiled and began limping away with Maria.

"I think Andy is the new Carlos," said Sasha.

"Ha!" blurted Willie. "Only he's a fuckin' pussy who pishes himself at the least sign of danger - and canny play a set of drums to save his life!" Willie shouted the last part out so that Andy could hear, but he and Maria continued on.

Without looking back, even once, they got into a jeep and drove away.

Sasha prised Willie's sleeve away to get a better look at his cut.

"Argh!" Willie pulled away from Sasha, and bumped into me.

"You are pussy, not him," snapped Sasha.

"What was that?" said Lorene.

"Just him, crying like baby," said Sasha, pointing at Willie and stepping back from him.

"No," said Lorene, "I heard something tinkle. Something metal."

We all scanned the ground.

"There," I said. I bent down and picked up a key. "It must have fallen out of my pocket when you pushed me." I gave Willie a glance, then picked up the Redante key. It was the one Maria had given me on Dead Dog Beach, but it looked strange.

"Let me see that," said Willie. He turned it over in his hands. "The bow is split."

The key had opened just enough to see something inside it.

I took it back from Willie and prized out a small piece of yellowed paper. It was covered in numbers.

Lorene tilted her head and said, "The old man on the beach told Maria the truth. The key did hold the secret."

"The four judges?" I said.

"That would be my guess," said Lorene. "These are co-ordinates."

"It might be enough to put all those idiots away for ever," said Willie. He pointed down towards the plumes of dust, way off in the distance.

"Maybe," I said closing my hand around the key. I pulled Lorene in close and she nuzzled into my neck.

"We better get you fixed up," she whispered.

Out of the corner of my eye I could see Willie slip his arm around Sasha but she pulled away from him.

"Fuck off, you smelly bastard!"

Willie ducked as she swung a punch at him. "What? I thought you liked me."

"I hate you," snapped Sasha.

They argued and swatted at each other all the way down to where the last of the jeeps were parked.

I moved forward to kiss Lorene but she hesitated. "Are you sure?"

"Totally sure," I said, pulling her in closer.

We kissed then looked down the rough incline at the quarrelling couple. I drew a heavy sigh and placed the key in my pocket. "Do you think we'll ever end up like that?"

A warm wind lifted the sand at our feet as Lorene smiled, her eyes bright with mischief. "I hope so."

About the Author

Paul James Murdoch lives by the River Clyde, Scotland, and
continues to appear at all sorts of cultural events
at home and abroad.
www.paulmurdoch.co.uk